ALL THE WILD HEARTS

A RED RIDING HOOD RETELLING

J.M. HACKMAN

ALL THE WILD HEARTS

A RED RIDING HOOD RETELLING

J.M. HACKMAN

To Chris, who never allowed me to give up.

Chapter One

I SAT CROSS-LEGGED ON the living room floor, staring into Mo's glowing green eyes. Whenever we held a staring contest, the family pet usually won since paszecs didn't need to blink as often. One of his gray furry ears twitched. With a low grunt, he tucked his short legs underneath his body. I didn't react. When his tail ghosted over my bare forearm, I jerked, the tickle breaking our game.

"Suns' halo, Mo." I stood. "You always cheat when we play."

The equivalent of a smirk played across his muzzle as his long whiskers quivered.

"Avarill? Don't forget the honey cakes for Mael." Grandma Hannah's reminder drifted down the steps from the second floor.

"I'll get them. Love you. See you tonight." I placed my dirty breakfast dishes in the PureScrub, so Grandma wouldn't have to do it later. Another cup of barzina would wake me up, but since the Meal Assembly System was broken, I didn't have time to make the creamy spiced drink. Already, the early morning sun streamed through the rock glass windows, highlighting the once-white walls and cluttered kitchen shelves.

After pulling on my boots, I slipped on my red shadowool cloak. The thick fabric kept my body heat close, just like a shadow, something I appreciated in Amaris's cold climate. The holes in the kitchen's cheap flooring exposed the aerogel insulation, but there was no money to repair it. We couldn't afford to fix the old pantry cabinets or the unpredictable Meal Assembly System, either, which only worked in warm weather. Equipped for the cold air outside, I pushed to my feet. Although the worn neo-res was small and basic, it was full of love. Grandma and I were a team and had been since my parents died three and a half years ago.

A jar of honey and two boxes of cooling pastries waited near the door, and I grabbed them before heading out into the chilly air.

The paszec escaped the house via the pet door and hopped around me, his tall ears twitching. Despite his two-foot stature, his luxuriant white and black tail flailed against my legs.

A surge of animal devotion and joy hit me, and I stroked between his furry ears. "Yes, I love you, too."

In the frosty morning light, Amaris's twin moons were faint spheres on the horizon. It'd been so hard to get up this morning. Fall had snuck into our village overnight, turning the temperate areas colder and coating everything with a thin rime of white. Behind the neo-res, the door to the glass house stood open. Frost bees flew from their protected hive inside to the last of the Echo Snowdrops blooming outside. A cheerful buzz filled the crisp air.

I made it to my wanderer parked beyond the glass house. The hovercar was the only thing I owned that was paid off. Dull black and rust-spotted, it wasn't pretty, but it was all mine.

Mo bumped into my knees, his square snout pushing me back toward the house. *Stay.*

"I can't, Mo." I gave him another scratch behind his ears.

The scent of sweet honey and roasted pecans wafted from the pastry boxes. Too bad there hadn't been extras. Mo and I could've split one. I loaded the boxes and the jar of honey into the back seat of the wanderer and climbed in.

Sadness in Mo's brilliant green eyes threatened to drown me, and his tail wilted. He bumped my knee again with his black, wet nose. "Buddy, I do this every day."

His eyes dimmed, and one of his ears drooped. I sighed. Being a fauna empath had its drawbacks. Family pets were masters at guilt.

"I'll be back tonight. Be a good boy." With one last rub, I shut the wanderer door.

My breath created white clouds in the freezing cockpit, and I snuggled into my red cloak. At least my vehicle had an enclosed control cabin. Some models on the market didn't, but a sealed cockpit was necessary here on the planet of Amaris.

I ran through a pre-flight checklist before turning on the de-icer and the heat. Unfortunately, I couldn't wait for the warmth. If there were too many deliveries, I'd finish after dark. My Primary Flight Display showed minimal aerial traffic, although the *CS Providence* was returning to the industrial sector. I always gave freighters a wide channel because of their size and the hazardous cargo. Cases of stardust energy, the volatile lifeblood of our solar system, filled their holds. The power source fueled everything from weaponry to homes to powerful artifacts. The extraction process left wisps of stardust in the atmosphere, the remnants painting the sky with beautiful colors of green, purple, and pink.

As the ice melted from my windshield, I flew toward the large district of Skift. To my far right and over the top of the next mountain lay the capital city of Cristalpeaks.

I'd been there once, when Grandma and I first arrived over three winters ago from the planet Ramilion. We'd worked hard to make the family farm work, but my parents had been the farmers. Their deaths, coupled with the planet's dry ground, had caused the farm to die, too. Grandma and I made the tough decision to move here and start over.

Cristalpeaks' urban landscape, crowds of tourists, and festive atmosphere had been a culture shock after our humble desert village. Crowds of people barhopped, shopped, ate, and partied in the cultural hub. I much preferred the slower pace of Skift. Our mountain neo-res wasn't much, but it was ours. Or at least it would be once we paid off the bank loan. While I enjoyed my delivery job, it was also one of the few ways I could help with the mortgage payment. Between my job and Grandma's profits from her honey business, we kept a roof over our heads.

My first stop was Fire and Ice Hearth. As I drew closer, I scanned the restaurant's cleared parking lot for a stomach-turning metallic wanderer. Nothing. Evading Wolfgang Vujic, resident creep and gray tycoon, made my delivery schedule more difficult. With a sigh of relief, I parked near the back door among the wanderers and snow cruisers.

After climbing out, I grabbed the boxes of cakes and a large jar of honey. A gust of wind flipped my pale blonde hair into my face. I climbed the ramp to the restaurant's back door, where the thin tin walls and roof of the small porch blocked most of the wind.

I put down the boxes of honey cakes and the honey and checked my BioDock, a communication device unit installed in my forearm. The only augmentation permitted for minors, it tracked vitals, sent communication messages, and allowed the user to buy and sell. Also powered by stardust, the units were in wide use across the Duo Soles solar system. While the poorest couldn't afford a device, my parents had scrimped and saved, installing one in me for my tenth birthday.

The loud roar from a landing vehicle filled the parking lot, and I rolled my eyes. *The loudest engine does not make you superior, ice cadet.*

Pickups and delivery requests scrolled across the comm screen. It was going to be another busy day. Turning off the BioDock, I raised a fist to knock on the back door. Familiar voices from the parking lot made me freeze.

"Order the billboard today, Kacic." Vujic's sharp voice, hard like new ice, made my stomach roll.

His closest associate spoke in a low rumble. "If we order the billboard, we won't be able to reschedule the opening. What if the shipment's late?"

"Do you know something I don't?"

"No, but we should get backup. Maybe a bear or lion, although it won't pull in as big a crowd."

I frowned. Why did Vujic want beasts like that?

"Our hunters are efficient and get paid well for what they do," Vujic said. "They'll deliver the first shipment on Friday. Are the crates ready?"

"The crew will finish building the last one tonight."

"Good job, Kacic. All I need to make my day a complete success will be to find that sexy delivery driver inside."

I pressed closer to the back entrance as if I could melt into the door.

"What's the draw with her?" his employee asked.

"She's beautiful."

"There are prettier girls in Cristalpeaks."

But not one who had turned him down as consistently as I did.

"I need her for my new business venture."

I almost swallowed my tongue. Which one? The business-man had his fingers in several illegal enterprises.

"Where are you going to put her?"

"We could draw a larger crowd if we added her to our event. I'm sure our audience would appreciate her."

My nausea worsened at his vague answer.

"Boss, she wouldn't last one round."

"Don't underestimate her. After all, Wild found some interesting information buried in her files."

Files? Cold that had nothing to do with the wind slipped down my neck. No, it was impossible. My parents had buried that information so deep it would take years to find it.

Kacic asked one of the key questions on my mind. "Who's Wild?"

"A talented codestitcher. I'd like to bring him on staff as well."

My heart plummeted to my boots. There was no way some techy ice cadet had burrowed deep enough into my past to find the one moment that changed me and my life.

"Avarill will be an entertaining addition to our main events on the weekends. Especially if she displays those assets she keeps covered up."

Shoving aside my disgust, I squeezed my eyes shut. Their laughter faded as they walked away. What had the codestitcher found? It couldn't be my secret. My parents had wiped the records after the surgery, even paying for "misplaced" files.

The small voice in my head started muttering. *He doesn't know what you can do, and he can't make you do anything. Just stay away from him, keep your head down, and your mouth shut.* Despite all the good advice, if Vujic wanted to talk to me, I could only avoid him for so long.

Suppressing a shiver, I knocked on the door.

Tommy, Mael's nephew, opened the door, his brown eyes sparkling. "Hey, Ava."

"Hi, Tommy. I've got Mael's order—two dozen honey cakes and a jar of Hannah's Honey."

"Mmm." He gave the air an appreciative sniff. "Come on in."

Sleek metallic shelves stacked with food stuff lined the hallway. The scents of Mael's Fire Ale and his famous potato and sausage stew drifted from the nearby kitchen. My mouth watered. As Tommy took the honey cakes into the storage area, Mael stepped to my side. His friendly grin displayed his missing front teeth, and a stained apron spanned his enormous belly. "Ah, Hannah's honey cakes, my best seller."

"Fresh this morning." I flipped open the protective shield of my BioDock.

Mael waved a silicon disc over the BioDock's screen, and a soft beep sounded as the funds transferred.

He handed me a sealed box the size of my fist. "Can you drop this off at DuoSolutions? Tommy jammed the store's payment dock, and it stopped working. Now I'm back to cash only." He shook his head, frowning.

"Sure." I hid a wince and typed in the business's address. Tommy would have to work twice as hard to make up for a mistake like that.

Moving closer, the big man dropped his voice. "Wolfgang Vujic just walked in. He's asking about you."

I swallowed hard. "Please don't tell him I'm here."

Mael squinted, his gaze concerned. "Are you messed up in something?"

"Of course not. You know me better than that." I'd turned down four dates, one marriage proposal, and more sexual innuendos than Grandma had bees, all delivered with his oily smile.

Mael patted my shoulder with a meaty hand. "Good for you. I couldn't imagine his money would turn your head."

Nothing could make me deal with Wolfgang Vujic. Not that it mattered. He always seemed to find me, but since he hadn't become physical, I couldn't report him.

"Better get going. I'll hold him off."

With a smile, I edged toward the door. "Thanks."

I breathed a little easier for the rest of the day, knowing Vujic had more important things to do than follow me around Skift. Even gray crime lords had a to-do list—people to threaten, businesses to demolish, puppies to kick.

I reflected on the conversation I'd overheard. I wasn't sure why the authorities didn't arrest Vujic. He owned bars, brothels, and casinos. No doubt political bribes and energy smuggling padded his resume, as well. Everyone knew he was crooked, but the authorities always trailed one step behind.

From the conversation I overheard, it appeared he was dipping a toe into the world of hunting apex predators, many of which were protected by environmental laws. Why did he need them? Sunspotted ideas, as distracting as mountain flies, flitted through my mind while I completed requested transports and deliveries. Maybe he was setting up a zoo or a traveling circus or a nature preserve, some innocuous-looking place to launder money. But he'd suggested adding me to a main event on the weekends. A lump formed in my stomach.

I pushed aside the unpleasant thoughts. After using my BioDock to comm Grandma to tell her to eat without me, I grabbed a supper bar from a traveling kiosk, then finished my deliveries.

Since many customers needed me to make a delivery for them, it'd been a profitable, albeit long, day. The double suns slipped to the horizon, the morning frost a distant memory.

As I flew to my last drop-off, warm lights shone from the houses. Polaris Mountain was charming in a wilderness kind of way, full of crags, forests, and trails. It might not have the opulence or glamorous night life of Cristalpeaks, but it was pretty in its own right.

A quarter mile from home, I settled the wanderer at the wealthy community of Winter Sun. The small village was built on Polaris Mountain's gentle slope. Seventy-five neo-reses spread out on one-acre lots nestled in a clearing. Large walnut trees lined the front boundaries, and the forest formed the back property line.

I parked near the forest at the first residence and climbed out. Close to a sticky chestnut tree, the twilight highlighted an unusual animal track—an imprint of a circular pad topped by four long slashes. Whatever it was, its claws were impressive. I scanned the shadowed tree line and waited, feeling a half dozen emotions from the animals hidden among the trees. One was hungry, another felt safe in its den, still another wary at my presence.

Silence fell as I approached the porch steps. The lights were off, no sounds came from inside. I stood still for a retinal scan, then a hatch near the exterior door trim opened. I dropped the bagged package inside. The cold wouldn't hurt the flat box of paper.

As I turned back toward my wanderer, the hair on my nape prickled. Confusion swamped me, and I stumbled. Pausing, I waited for the sensation to clear. My hands shook as a hot pressure gripped my chest. This occasionally happened when an animal in distress was nearby, but this time, my response was overpowering.

A growl came from behind my vehicle, and an animal stepped into view.

The head was a mountain lion, but the body shape was twisted and deformed. The powerful torso connected to an emaciated stomach. Its visible ribs covered with fur led to eight spindly legs ending in taloned paws.

Waves of emotion battered me. Anger, confusion, and hunger—I couldn't think through the creature's feelings. It blocked the path to my vehicle, and a locked residence lay behind me. The lights next door were on, and I sidled toward its porch steps.

Whining, the spider-lion scuttled closer, and the pitiful sound gripped my heart.

"I won't hurt you," I tried in a calm voice.

The creature paused and growled. I sent him comforting images of warm dens and savanna grasses. Confusing static filled my mind. Lowering his head, he stalked toward me. A cold sweat chilled my back.

"Hello?" I called, hoping for a rescue from someone, anyone, nearby. "Help? Please?"

Never looking away from the animal, I continued to move toward the illuminated house. I stumbled as a wave of vertigo hit.

With a savage snarl, the creature lunged for me.

Screaming, I turned and ran.

The animal slipped and slid, crunching through the snow behind me. I'd never make it to the safety of the house.

The front door flew open as the creature knocked me down. I rolled, and a powerful paw slammed into my chest, thumping the air from my lungs. My cloak had slipped to the side, and the creature's claw punctured my red thermic shirt. Its hot breath hit my face.

Hoping the element of surprise would allow me to escape, I waved my arm and screamed, "Go away!"

Two more legs struck, pinning my left arm and leg. My eyes widened. It snarled, its pointed teeth like knives. One heartbeat, then it lunged. I flung up my free arm to protect my throat. The knives sunk into my forearm.

I shrieked, pain streaking from my arm to my neck.

"Get off," a male voice roared, an aggressive thunder of sound. A thud, then a snarl, and the pressure on my arm disappeared. I flinched, pain and horror wrapping around me. I curled into a ball and pulled the cloak over my head, the creature's terror mingling with my own. Through a slit in the material, I watched the animal bolt into the shadows.

Dead leaves and packed snow pressed against my cheek, and tremors took hold. I couldn't move as ice filled my veins.

Chapter Two

Blaiz

BLOOD DRENCHED THE GIRL's forearm. She held her cloak over her head as if the material would protect her, while dark crimson rivulets stained the cloth. I touched a shaking shoulder, and she recoiled.

"Hoarfrost," I muttered. "Don't move."

She lowered the cloak to meet my gaze but didn't respond. Bits of brown leaves tangled in her messy white-blonde hair, and melting snow clung to a pale cheek. I eyed her injury. No skin or fabric was missing, but my first aid kit was inside. I couldn't leave her out here alone.

My spirit wolf stirred, whined. The augmented desire to protect shoved to the forefront of my mind. *Shelter. Help.* "I'll have to carry you. You're injured."

When she simply blinked, I took the action as permission and lifted her.

She gasped. Her next breath was a stifled sob behind gritted teeth.

Cupping her elbow, she drew her arm closer to her body and laid her head onto my shoulder. A chilly wind brushed past my cheek, carrying the faint scent of snow. The crisp perfume of winter pears and the metallic tang of blood overwhelmed it. I secured my grip and bolted up the shallow porch steps leading into my house.

The warmth of the augmented reality fire in the fireplace surrounded us. My oasis, simple and comfortable, was decorated in warm tones of russet and green. A floor-to-ceiling bookshelf covered one wall, while a massive dimensional laserscreen took up the other wall. A state-of-the-art two-tier keyboard and a humming server flanked the wide blue grid.

The girl slitted open her eyes. Blue, like Echo Snowdrops. I repressed a snort. The poetic thought was so unlike me, it was obvious I needed sleep. Or a cup of barzina. Or a reality check.

Bypassing the stuffed chairs, I placed her on a hunter green couch. Her injured arm faced out, and the position kept the laserscreen at her back. Her blonde hair framed her pale face, and rigid lines bracketed her full mouth. If a toxin was affecting her, I was losing valuable time, standing and staring at her.

The thought galvanized me. "Don't move. I'll get something to stop your bleeding."

Hurrying into the kitchen, I returned with the first aid kit and a damp cloth. She set her jaw and tried to scoot up, but I laid a hand on her shoulder with a small smile. "Relax. I don't want blood on my sofa."

My teasing fell flat, and she dropped her chin to her chest. Great, I'd embarrassed her. Biting my tongue, I pulled up a footstool to her side and sat.

After pulling back her sleeve to examine her wound, I looked up. The intensity of her gaze speared through me. A rose blush tinted her cheeks, and she glanced away. Was she checking me out? Probably not. Injured and in pain, she didn't need a DNA anomaly like me coming on to her. Anyone could sense the predator lurking just under my skin.

"I'm Blaiz Weylin," I offered. "Sorry I didn't introduce myself sooner.".

She shook her head. "I was distracted, you know, trying not to get killed. I'm Avarill Engel."

Her name stunned like an electric shock, but I forced my face to remain blank. What were the chances we'd meet, even like this? I'd never met my marks, didn't care to meet people who were like my father. I removed a square of antiseptic sponge, a topical antibiotic serum packet, and a sheet of Restorscreen from the first aid kit. She looked nothing like the criminals I used to deal with. She probably used those big blue eyes and her pretty face to her advantage before realizing that wouldn't work with Vujic.

Once I soaked up the blood, I opened the packet. "That's a deep bite."

"I'd be dealing with more than just a bite if you hadn't come along." She hissed through her teeth as I swabbed the wound with serum.

My inner wolf whined at her discomfort. "Well, your skin didn't tear. Even though it looked like that creature had a firm grip on your arm, these are just punctures."

I placed the sheet of Restorscreen on the wound. When I pressed on the edges to seal it, she whimpered.

"Sorry. I'll get a physipad."

I strode into the bathroom and searched for the physipad in the storage closet. My wolf whined again, desperate to ease her pain. His protective instinct and my human concern swirled in my chest. I'd relieve her pain and send her on her way. A sudden thought rose. How could I treat an animal bite I couldn't even identify? If there was venom or poison present, she'd be in trouble. For now, she seemed stable, just in pain from the bite. Finding the physipad hidden under a stack of clean towels, I grabbed it and walked back to her side.

While she rested, I scanned her with the device, setting it for pain removal, sterilizing, and skin regen. The small tablet beeped, the report appearing on screen.

[MINIMAL BLOOD LOSS. VENOM: NEGATIVE.]

[STAPHYLOCOCCUS AND PASTEURELLA MULTOCIDA BACTERIA NEUTRALIZED.]

[KEEP WOUND COVERED.]

As the warm healing power flowed over her body, the tension slid away from her face.

I sat on the stool, stuffing my curiosity down deep where it belonged. I couldn't get drawn into the criminal underworld after I'd crawled my way out. No interrogation, no peeling back her layers. Although Vujic was no saint, he could deal with this con artist. My inner wolf huffed in disagreement, letting his preference be known.

Frowning, I ignored him. We would sit here in silence until she felt well enough to leave. Despite my best efforts, the next words out of my mouth were, "Do you usually explore the woods in the dark?"

With a glower, she nodded toward the view of the top of Polaris Mountain through my living room window. "When I have to. I live on the mountain and do deliveries for my grandmother and others in Skift. She owns Hannah's Honey."

I grunted. She had a legitimate job? "The honey cakes Mael sells at the restaurant are really good."

"Well, I just gave him a fresh delivery today. You better hurry there if you want one." She winced as she stretched her arm. "It's a little tender, but I think I can vacate your couch."

My eyes widened. With that injury, completing more errands wasn't a good idea. She needed to recover. Of course, that was the real reason. "Listen, snowdrop. You can't run around with a wound like that."

"I'm heading home."

"What if it bleeds again?"

Her mouth pressed into a thin line. "Then I'll apply another sheet of Restorscreen."

Stubborn. My inner wolf growled, but I covered it with a cough. "There's still that creature out there." I shook my head. "What was that thing?"

"I have no clue. It was like a cross between a lion and a furred spider. I've never seen anything like that."

If I hadn't been here to help Avarill, she'd be dead. My chest tightening, I rubbed my sternum. "Yet it attacked you like a lion. Did you provoke it?"

Shooting me a glare, she sat up. "Yes, I regularly kick wild animals. Of course not. It was just scared and hungry. And furious."

I paused at her slip. Although I shouldn't, I knew what she was talking about.

An awkward silence fell, and she rushed to fill it. "I think. You know, 'cause it was snarling...and stuff."

Of course, she'd try to hide an ability like hers. It was a little too late, since I'd found her secret and passed it along to Vujic like he'd asked. You couldn't cross a gray tycoon like Vujic and expect to come out on top.

I raised an eyebrow. "How, by all the ice demons, can you tell what an animal's feeling?"

Her gaze danced around the room, never lighting on one thing for long. Her fingers twisted in her lap. "I was just guessing. Not that I'd know, right? I mean, that'd be sunspotted."

"You know, I can always tell when someone's lying. And you're not good at it. At all." I almost missed the hint of desperation that crossed her expression.

"I think what you're seeing on my face is pain, not dishonesty," she said.

"It's not just your expression, it's your gestures. The way you can't sit still, and you're biting your lip. Tell me how you knew what that animal was feeling, snowdrop."

She froze like a glacier, although her scowl burned. "One, my name isn't snowdrop. And two, its body language told me everything I needed to know."

"It pinned you and was growling. That's fear. But hunger and anger?"

"Anger and fear present the same. The hunger is obvious. Didn't you notice its ribs? It was starving."

With an ability like hers, I'd keep my secrets, too. If the government learned she could communicate with animals, her life would no longer be her own. At best, she'd become an animal behavioral consultant. If she fell into corrupt hands, she might become someone's lab rat, being subjected to ever-worsening tests. Con woman or not, no one deserved that fate.

Clearing my throat, I backed off. "You must be an animal behaviorist."

Her gaze slid away. "It's a hobby of mine."

I frowned. Despite her obvious lie, she had a wide-eyed innocence that didn't seem to match what Vujic had told me. Her gaze met mine, the sour tang of fear mixing with interest as her eyes widened. My wolf waited under the surface, but I pushed him down. *Back off. We don't protect criminals. We're the good guys now.*

This girl was already messing with my control more than I liked. Like most animals, my shadow wolf was an excellent judge of people, and he was urging me to protect her. But I'd dealt with cons for years, and I wasn't getting mixed up with another, no matter how pretty she was.

An ember in the fireplace popped. She straightened and slid forward on the couch. "I didn't say so, but thank you for helping."

"I'm glad it took off when I smacked it with that two by four." A sudden thought occurred to me. "You know, I wonder if that creature is from SpliceSystems' accident. You heard about that, right?"

The company, proponents of genetic engineering, had launched a program combining DNA with star energy, but quality control had become an issue. When the accident occurred four months ago, pictures of the crash flooded the news feeds. Official statements warned the shipment of laced wildlife had escaped from the transport vehicle upon impact. SpliceSystems personnel advised extreme caution before offering compensation to those who captured the animals.

"Yeah. If so, you missed your opportunity to be ten thousand puli richer," she said.

As if I needed more money. "I'm not interested in capturing an apex predator like that."

Her cheeks paled at my words.

Inside my chest, the wolf jerked to attention, and I shifted closer. "You look like you just had the worst thought in the Duo Soles system."

"Did they ever catch all of them?"

"Out of the ten, they only found two."

With a hard swallow, she rubbed her stomach, her expression dragging her to some fear-filled nightmare.

I frowned. "What's wrong?"

"Nothing. I should go."

"Remember what I told you earlier? You're a lousy liar."

Keeping her face turned away, she stood from her spot on the couch. "I'm tired. It's been a long day."

"Come on. If you tell me what's wrong, maybe I can help." I couldn't seem to resist the urge, even if it was the worst thing I could do.

Taking a hasty step toward the door, she wrapped her coat around her. "Thanks so much for the first aid and letting me recover here. I—"

"Avarill?" I stood. She hadn't recovered enough. She needed to stay. *Forever*, my wolf added. Dumb animal.

She didn't stop, her steps taking her toward the door. "—hope I didn't get blood on your couch, but if I did, contact me, and—"

"Avarill."

"—I'll pay you *backthanksbye*."

The door slammed shut behind her.

Through my living room window, I watched her run to her vehicle. Something had her terrified. It was probably me. She'd sensed the predator and escaped.

Help her. My inner wolf's idea was laughable. According to Vujic, she owed him money. There was no way out when someone got on the bad side of the man.

I shook my head. The best I could do for Avarill was to stay far away from her—if my wolf would let me.

Chapter Three

AVARILL

I ROLLED OVER IN bed and groaned. A warm wall of fur stopped me mid-roll, and I pulled my head back so I could breathe. Mo often climbed into bed with me when the weather turned colder. I stroked a long ear before adding a scratch at his ruff with my good arm and snuggled under the butter yellow comforter. After a few more minutes of rest, I sat up and pushed the blankets down. All my clothes lay in a heap on the floor, minus my cloak. I'd run it through the ion cleaner twice before I went to bed last night. Thankfully, no sign of the bloodstains remained.

Late morning sunlight seeped past the thin shields of my bedroom, creating warm gold spots on the floor and cream walls. A slight chill filled the small room as the building's nanosensors directed the warmth to the living areas downstairs. On weekdays, I didn't sleep in, but today was Saturday. A guy with two-tone brown hair and an intense amber gaze had filled my dreams. Blaiz Weylin. Too bad I'd never see him again, not unless he needed an item picked up or delivered.

My injured arm had scabbed over, but it ached. The creature had put pounds of force into the bite, gifting me with a lovely multicolor rainbow.

When I arrived home late last night, Grandma was waiting up for me. I downplayed the attack so she wouldn't worry and treated the wound myself with a fresh sheet of Restorscreen. It felt a little better this morning. I hadn't mentioned my idea about the laced animals or Vujic. There was no proof or evidence of my theory.

A low voice drifted up the stairs from the first floor, and I froze, my feet turning icy on the cold floor. Was Vujic downstairs? I tiptoed closer to the stairwell to listen. No, his voice was sharp. This baritone voice was smooth like cream, perfect for soothing a frightened child, or convincing a person to buy a block of ice mid-winter. Relief trickled through me.

Mo stiffened, his long ears swiveling. *Stranger. Play.* With a muffled cluck, he skidded over to my bedroom door and looked back, as if waiting for me. He loved greeting Grandma's customers who came for jars of honey and viewed them as opportunities for play and head pats.

"Not yet, Mo. I'm not going down there in my pajamas."

The paszec huffed and settled, his backside twitching.

After using a physipad to ease my aches, I got dressed in a pair of warm black pants, a fuzzy cobalt sweater, and thick socks. I left my hair down. Thick and glossy, my hair slipped out of ponytails and buns, as if it had a mind of its own. At least it kept my neck warm.

Mo had escaped minutes ago, too excited to wait for me. I took the curved stairs down to the first floor. In the stairwell hung flixers of me and Grandma this summer, as well as several of my parents, their animated smiles so real, yet captured in the past. I followed the scent of honey cakes through the living room. The sun shone through the open shields, highlighting the worn furnishings. A fuzzy cream throw hung across the back of the overstuffed hoverchair. Grandma's arthritis often forced her to sleep on the first floor. The sight in the kitchen halted me in the archway.

Blaiz sat at the counter, eating a honey cake with an enormous glass of milk. He looked up and studied me. "Morning. How do you feel after last night?"

Grandma didn't give me time to answer. "Blaiz told me all about that terrible attack."

I blinked. "Do you two know each other?"

"He stopped by to check on you this morning. You made it sound like nothing," she said.

"It is nothing. It's healing already, and I hardly feel it." As long as I was careful.

With a scowl, Blaiz held out a hand. "Let me see."

I ignored the demand and moved to plate up my breakfast at the scarred counter. "I'm not a toddler."

After pouring myself a mug of barzina, I sprinkled the creamy drink with a pinch of milfoil glow for some spice. I slid a still-warm honey cake onto my plate and turned. The only place left to sit was next to Blaiz. His amber eyes tracked me.

I sat next to him and closed my eyes to thank Kethiran for another meal, but a faint hint of clean mint and fresh snow distracted me. I opened my eyes and shot a quick glance at Blaiz. Had he moved closer?

"You're not a toddler, but you're acting like one," he said.

Excuse me? I glared. "What's that supposed to mean?"

"It means you're being rude to your grandmother. She cares about you. Not everyone has that." A muscle jumped in his jaw as he turned back to his breakfast.

"There's nothing wrong with asking for help," Grandma stated with a pointed frown in my direction.

The reprimand stung. Whose side was she on? I didn't need this first thing in the morning. I took a drink of barzina, the milfoil warming my throat.

Before I could provide a defense or an apology, she bustled toward the door. "I'm going to check the hives."

How rude for Blaiz to level accusations that were... I sighed. They were true.

I glanced at him. "You're right, okay? Sorry. I'm used to taking care of myself."

Blaiz sat back, his expression unreadable. "Asking for help doesn't make you weak. It makes you human."

I turned to my breakfast, unable to think with him next to me. His presence tied my stomach in knots, interest and nerves battling inside.

As I took a big bite of the honey cake, the moist crumbs melted in my mouth. Mo stationed himself next to my chair, his long white whiskers quivering. Even if I couldn't see it on his face, hopefulness radiated from him in waves. I caved, dropping a small bite for him.

Blaiz's voice broke the silence. "Do you have any deliveries today?"

"No, Saturdays and Sundays are my off days. What about you? I never asked what you did."

A muscle ticced in his jaw. "I have a small computer service business."

The huge, blue-gridded laserscreen flashed in my memory. "It didn't look small. I saw the enormous set up in your living room."

With a shrug, Blaiz studied his glass of milk. "It pays the bills."

He still hadn't met my gaze. My stomach gave an unusual shiver, and I shifted in my chair. Why was he self-conscious? Was the business still struggling? Something told me I shouldn't have asked, although the jittery nervousness tightening my shoulders didn't make sense. I looked at Mo, who was still waiting for crumbs. Was this strange feeling from the paszec? I brushed off the sensation—maybe it was an animal outside the cabin.

"Well, I think it's pretty solar to have a useful skill like that. Maybe if I did..." I shrugged. The delivery job wouldn't make us rich, but it paid enough.

He raised an eyebrow. "Yeah? What if you did have a skill like that?"

"I could make more money to help pay off our mortgage. Maybe fix the broken Meal Assembly System or replace the kitchen floor."

His brow wrinkled, but I turned away to finish my breakfast. My heart squeezed a bit when Blaiz shared his last bite of cake with Mo.

He propped a forearm on the counter, definitely not leaving, and leaning in close to my personal space. "You never answered my question last night."

Suns' halo, he smelled good—it was like sitting in a mint garden, the air crisp with an incoming storm. All I wanted to do was move into his arms and inhale his delicious scent.

Blinking at the intimate thought, I removed my breakfast dishes from the counter. My blood sugar must be wonky. "What question?"

Before he could answer, there was a knock at the door. Mo jumped from his place and thumped one of his powerful back legs twice. *Stranger.*

"It's probably a buyer who wants a custom order. Can you get Grandma Hannah, please?" I asked Blaiz as I moved toward the front door.

Relief flooded me as he left to find her. He was too distracting. I'd meant what I'd said—taking care of myself and Grandma was what I was used to. I'd deal with Wolfgang Vujic the same way, although in the bright light of morning, some of my fear and curiosity about the businessman's comments faded.

When I opened the door, Vujic stood on the porch. Gray threaded through the dark hair at his temples, but his forehead was unlined. His mouth stretched into a smile, his teeth whiter than a three-day blizzard. "Hello, Avarill."

My heart rocketed into my throat. "What do you want?"

Grunting, Mo splayed his short legs. *Fear. Danger. Warning.*

His blue eyes glittered like stolen sapphires. "My, my, such uncharitable behavior."

I threw out a surge of calming influence, and Mo sat at my feet.

Vujic smoothed his coat with a well-manicured hand. "If you allow me to come in, I have important information to share with you and your grandmother."

Although I debated letting him stand in the cold, an icy rush of air decided for me. I moved back to let him step inside.

"Wolfgang Vujic, what are you doing in my home?" Grandma Hannah had returned from the hives and stood behind me, her hands on her hips. Blaiz was nowhere to be seen.

"There have been a few recent developments regarding your mortgage." Vujic unbuttoned his expensive shadowool coat and scanned our living room. He assessed the worn rugs, faded upholstery, and ancient furniture with a critical eye. But it was ours. We didn't need anything extravagant like the platinum-plated BioDock peeking out from under his jacket cuff.

Grandma crossed her arms. "What are you talking about?"

He ignored her question as his gaze slid down my body. I tried to suppress the shudder that shook me. Mo offered another high-pitched snuffle and leaned against my side, letting me know he was there to protect me.

"I bought your residence loan from the bank. I'm your new landlord. Your mortgage will be due in full at the end of the month."

My mouth fell open as I leaned back against the wall. We didn't have that kind of money.

Grandma lifted her chin. "That's ridiculous. We don't have the income to pay off the mortgage that quickly."

Vujic smiled again. "That's unfortunate, but I have a solution. I have a job for you, Avarill."

"I already have a job."

"Taking this employment opportunity would be in your best interest."

The statement sounded like a threat, just like he intended. Still, I shook my head. "What I have suits me just fine, thanks."

"Unfortunately, I must insist. This one caters specifically to your talents."

At his last three words, my stomach dropped to my feet. I wanted to live a quiet life, just making deliveries in Skift. Maybe that's all he needed—a delivery driver for sensitive information. Wrapping my arms around myself, I gripped my elbows.

He continued with a smirk. "If you come work for me, we can work out an agreeable payment plan. I'm starting a new business venture, and your income would be more than adequate. You'll be the perfect assistant."

His voice caressed the last sentence, and my breath turned choppy. He had me cornered, but I couldn't let Grandma lose the house. It was all we had.

Grandmother frowned. "What kind of business? My grand-daughter is a good girl."

"Of course she is. Her virtue won't be compromised." His expression, as if my worth was trivial, made my hands curl into fists.

She marched to the door and held it open, her gaze hard. "Thank you for the information. We need time to discuss your offer."

Vujic tossed a glossy black business card onto the coffee table before moving to the door. "Contact me if you have questions. Make your decision by next week. I'll be in touch. Good day."

He was gone in a breeze of expensive cologne that burned my nose.

Grandma slammed the door behind him. "I wouldn't trust that man even if all the ice on Amaris melted."

My stomach flipping, I ignored the lump in the back of my throat. It was time to think up a side hustle that would create oodles of money out of nothing.

She turned to me. "Ava, don't listen to a word that man says. We'll manage just fine."

"How?" My voice was small.

Grandma set her jaw. "Kethiran will present the right opportunity. Don't worry."

I had no faith a divine opportunity existed. Rather than argue, I peered into the kitchen. "Where's Blaiz?"

"Hmm, he must've gone home. He said he had some things to do."

I pressed my lips together. Blaiz's departure wasn't surprising. Vujic had a way of clearing a room. And although a part of me wished Blaiz had stayed, at least he hadn't met Vujic. The less time spent with Vujic, the better.

Chapter Four

AVARILL

THE NEXT DAY, Mo followed me outside. We trekked up one of the small trails threading through the woods behind our house. We didn't go far, but the chilly air cleared my head. A thick layer of snow had fallen overnight, coating the ground, bushes, and trees in fluffy white. A heavy gray sky promised more snow. Near the edge of the forest, bunny tracks marred the surface. Although the animal hid nearby, its wariness increased before I walked past. Two blue-winged woodpeckers tapped at a nearby tree, their staccato taps urgent as they searched for insects.

I stayed on the trail, my feet finding the path with ease. It ended in a clearing, offering a view of Skift proper. I sat on a large rock, a perfect thinking spot, while Mo romped through the snow, looking for wildlife pals to play with.

Vehicles zoomed overhead. Their lights left white trails like comets. Several floating billboards drifted over the town, and the dark suspended building of Answers Corporation rested in the sky, the offices of wealthy businessmen.

Below lay residences with gleaming photovoltaic roofs. A couple of burnished church spires rose between the places of business where I'd delivered packages. The town looked like a glistening paradise with its new carpet of snow. Underneath lay corrupt businesses run by Vujic. Nothing he oversaw was legitimate, despite the respectable façade displayed for the ignorant citizens.

Last night, sleep eluded me as I'd replayed his words and looked for an escape. This morning had produced no solutions.

I was still pondering the problem when Blaiz broke into the clearing where I sat. He strolled over, his breath puffing out in clouds in the brisk air.

"Your grandma mentioned you were up here," he said, burying his hands in his jacket pockets.

"It's a great place to think and clear your head." It just hadn't worked for me this time.

Blaiz settled next to me on the rock. "I heard about your visitor. I didn't realize you were friends."

"We aren't. He likes to come by and harass us."

His brow furrowed. "I should've been there."

"No, you don't want to get mixed up with him. He's—he's not a nice guy," I finished.

"I know who he is and what he's capable of."

I shot him a glance. I didn't know Blaiz well. Maybe he'd had a run-in with Vujic before.

"My brother, Bran, works for the peacekeeping force for Cristalpeaks and the surrounding towns," he said, as if reading my mind. "They receive reports about the illegal deals Vujic is involved in, but they can't get the evidence. Why is he so intent on you?"

My laugh was hollow. "Just lucky, I guess. It started off as a minor annoyance. He asked me out a couple times, which I turned down."

"He's old enough to be your father," Blaiz muttered.

"Yeah, I know. He didn't take the hint. Then he proposed, which I also turned down. When he realized he wasn't getting

anywhere, he'd stalk me or make crude comments whenever
he saw me."

"That's sexual harassment."

I gave a shrug. "He can't be arrested for that."

A muscle jumped in Blaiz's jaw as he glared at the view of
the town. "That's it?"

"Isn't that enough?"

"I meant, do you owe him money or—?"

"No." I swallowed hard. "Although I've been avoiding him
as much as possible, last night he offered me a job. I don't
think he's used to hearing the word no. Which makes me
wonder how he'll handle my rejection of his job offer."

Blaiz frowned. "You're turning him down?"

"I'm going to do whatever I can to avoid working for him.
But we can't lose the house, and Grandma isn't in good
enough health to pick up another job."

Saying the bare facts out loud was terrifying. It was all up to
me. I took a couple of deep breaths to manage the worry. The
warmth of Blaiz's shoulder seeped into mine. For a ridiculous
second, I felt safe.

"What about a savings account?"

The secure feeling evaporated. An icy breeze smelling of
an incoming front sent a shiver down my neck. "Blaiz, there
isn't anything else. There's no magic bullet, or surprise trust
fund, or safety net. The house is *all we have*." I stressed the
last three words as my eyes stung.

He studied my face. "When does he expect an answer?"

"Next week."

"Don't give him an answer until you absolutely have to."

I shot him a skeptical look. "Why?"

The chilly wind ruffled his hair as he gazed at the town
below. "I have an idea or two, but I need a little more time."

"Blaiz, no. This isn't your battle. Grandma and I will figure something out." The words were as flimsy as they sounded.

"Do you want to work for Vujic?"

"Absolutely not, but I don't—"

"Then let me help. Remember, you're not weak, just human."

I finally nodded my head. "Okay. If you come up with anything that saves our house and keeps me away from him, you're a miracle worker."

Emotions rushed across Blaiz's face so fast I couldn't identify them. The memory of our conversation stayed with me, but I knew—Grandma and I were on our own.

A day later, Blaiz stopped by after my deliveries. Grandma had headed to the glass house to check the frost bees, leaving Blaiz and me alone in the living room.

"Have you and your grandmother talked about Vujic's offer?" he asked as he sat in the stuffed chair next to me.

I shifted on the couch, avoiding a broken spring. "No, not yet. She's still expecting a perfect opportunity to come along. Maybe there's something I haven't thought of yet." Although I doubted it. Maybe a wanderer would run over Vujic some morning.

Mo snuggled next to me on the couch and laid his head on my lap. *Home?* I gave him a half smile, scratching behind his long ear. "No, buddy, we won't lose our home. We'll get through this."

With a grunt, Mo licked my hand, his answer to the anxiety filling my chest every time I thought about our new landlord.

Blaiz leaned forward, and I realized what I'd done. Suns' halo. Maybe he'd ignore it.

"Did he ask you a question?"

My heart racing, I shook my head. The paszec picked up on it, and another grunt escaped him. I squashed my unease and scratched his ear again. "Shh, buddy," I said in a low voice.

Mo dropped his head back to my lap but continued to face Blaiz.

Blaiz studied me. "And he responds to you. It's like an actual conversation. Are you able to do this with any animal or just Mo?"

A surgery ten years ago had saved my life but also left me unlike any other person on the planet. I kept my ability to myself, only sharing it with family and close friends I could trust.

He was still waiting for an answer. My mind raced with excuses, and I shook my head. "No, you've got it all wrong. He's just extremely intelligent."

I didn't give Blaiz a chance to respond. "Hey, speaking of intelligent, do you want to see the frost bee hives?"

Hopping to my feet, I headed for the door, not really caring if Blaiz was following me or not. The cold air cooled my warm cheeks, and I pushed our uncomfortable conversation aside. I wanted to trust Blaiz, but my parents had drilled it into me—trust no one. Maybe one day I could tell him, but not yet.

"And are they? Intelligent, I mean."

"They're one of the smartest insects on the planet. They work hard and contribute to the hive, like an enormous family."

Mo followed at my feet, my constant friend and protector.

Grandma was behind the glass house, mending a hive frame. The door to the glass house was open, as usual. We only closed it at night.

Blaiz lingered at the doorway, but I waved him in. "Don't worry, they won't sting."

He lifted an eyebrow. "Are you sure about that?"

I smiled, the productive humming telling of a happy hive. "Frost bees are very docile insects."

A white bee landed on my arm, and I held it up to show Blaiz. "This worker bee collects pollen from the Echo Snowdrops."

"The blue and purple flowers outside?"

Nodding, I pointed to the purplish dust on the bee's limbs. "If you look closely, you can see the pollen on his legs."

He froze like a statue as a bee landed on his chest for a moment and then flew off.

"Just relax. They won't hurt you." I eyed his tight jaw. "Are you scared of them?"

He blinked several times before waving away my words. "Of course not. I just don't know much about them."

"Good thing I'm here then. Follow me."

I led him further into the glass house, aiming for the coolest area in the far corner. "Frost bees thrive in cooler temperatures. So, we keep this area of the glass house shaded and temperature controlled. The frost bees do the rest."

"How?" he asked.

As we walked around the L-shaped set of cabinets where we strained and jarred the honey, the hive came into view. Mounted on the wall, the hives took up the ten-foot square area reserved for them. Spaced evenly apart, the three hives glittered, the ice cells filled with the unique blue honey.

"The workers that don't collect pollen build the hives with ice. It keeps the hives cool and preserves the honey. And of course, frost honey is the sweetest honey there is."

Blaiz took another step closer, his rigid shoulders softening as he studied the marvel of sparkling, symmetrical perfection. Sometimes, I'd search the cells in the hives, looking for differences, but each one was a flawless hexagon.

Grandma shuffled around the cabinets, holding a box full of glass jars. "Hello, you two."

"Mrs. Engle, let me carry that for you." He had it in his arms before I could blink.

Grandma wiped off her forehead with her hand. "Thank you, Blaiz. You can put the box over there on the collecting counter. And no need for formality. Just call me Grandma Hannah."

My brows rose. She only allowed people she really liked to call her that.

"What do you think of my bees?" she asked him.

He turned and studied the hives again. "Amazing. There aren't many places where you can find teamwork like this."

Grandma nodded. "The bees understand that, especially since fall is moving in. They're building up the last of their winter reserves."

"We'll be gathering the final honey flow soon," I said.

Blaiz looked at me then Grandma Hannah. "Do you need help? I have some free time."

My eyes widened. "You don't have to, you know. Especially if you're not comfortable around them."

"Hey, I want to help. Besides, how did you describe them? Docile?"

Grandma gave me a knowing smirk before answering. "That's a generous offer. I could send a couple jars home with you in payment."

He grinned, the smile making him look younger. "I can't turn that down."

"Wonderful. We can exchange comm numbers before you leave today, and I'll contact you with the collecting date," she said and headed out the door.

Blaiz watched the bees a little longer before we followed her inside to play a game of cards.

After two games of cards, Blaiz left. Our time together had been almost normal, just a friend hanging out. Well, an incredibly handsome friend hanging out, which wasn't normal for me at all.

My grandmother and I didn't discuss Vujic's offer. Time ticked away, but I still didn't have any idea how to escape. The next day, I worked late into the night, making as many deliveries as I could.

Grandma had already turned in for the evening, and Mo had curled up in the middle of my bed like the cover hog he was. Nudging him aside, I settled on the bed and stuck my stocking feet under the comforter to keep them warm. I counted my tips then added the amount to the digital puli entered in my BioDock. Tallying the total, I slumped back against the pillow. Maybe several more days would make a difference.

A sudden need to talk to my best friend Karis swept over me. She lived on the planet Ramilion, but we stayed in touch with comms. Setting the BioDock for audio only, I commed her number from memory. She answered seconds later.

"Ava!" she squealed.

"Hi, Karis." I grinned at her enthusiastic greeting.

"Wow. You're down about something."

"How can you tell?" I burrowed closer to Mo's furry side.

I could almost hear her roll her eyes. "Please. I'm your best friend. I know these things. What's wrong?"

"It's just been a tough week." I paused, but Karis waited me out. "We got a new landlord who raised our rent. I've had run-ins with him before, and now it looks like I might have to go to work for him just so we can keep the house."

"Is it the same danjaba quarkhead you mentioned before?"

I winced at the curse word. In the past, I'd told her about my previous unpleasant interactions with Vujic. "Yeah, same guy."

"That's terrible. I'm so sorry, Ava. I wish I could help."

"Hey, just talking to you helps." Karis's positive outlook usually cheered me up. "Besides, maybe Blaiz or I will come up with a way to avoid the situation."

"Blaiz? Who's that?" Her voice pitched up, full of curiosity.

I cleared my throat. "Oh, um, just a guy I met."

"Yeah? How? When?"

"A laced predator attacked me outside his house. He literally saved my life." I shook my head. It wasn't necessarily a meet-cute, but Blaiz would sound quite heroic in the retelling.

"Wow. I need to hear this."

I settled in, telling her about the strange creature, Blaiz's first aid, and how we seemed to be slowly developing a friendship.

"Just a friendship?" she asked.

My cheeks heated. "Not every new handsome guy has to be more than a friend, you know."

"Ooh, he's cute, too?"

I slapped my forehead, too tired to navigate my growing feelings about Blaiz and censor myself. After a few more minutes, I promised to comm later and signed off.

Although no problems were solved, I was happier and more relaxed after hearing Karis's voice.

Over the next three days, Blaiz sent short comms to say hi, but I was still working long hours, picking up deliveries farther away than I ever had. At the end of the third day, I was on my way home when he commed. The moons Joya and Jesek were sinking toward the horizon, a sign I only had several hours before dawn arrived. "Are you home?" he asked without a hello.

I yawned. "Not yet. On my way. Did you need a delivery or something?"

He uttered a curse. "I wouldn't tell you even if I did. You're working too hard."

"The money won't show up on its own, Blaiz. But if I extend my hours to Saturday and Sunday, maybe—"

"Ava, stop. You're exhausted."

"How do you know?" Another yawn snuck up on me, and I muffled it behind my hand. "I haven't seen you for days."

"I commed your grandmother yesterday. We're both worried about you."

"Don't be. I'm fine. I'm home now. Have to go." Signing off, I parked the wanderer and stumbled inside.

An hour later, I stared at the dark shadows in my room as Mo snored beside me. Even if I continued to pull long hours, it wouldn't be enough. Yesterday, I'd made a list of things I could sell or side jobs I could do. The dismally short list said nothing would bring in enough money to make the new payments.

Several days later, Vujic stopped by. He didn't knock and wait politely. He just walked in, like he owned the place. My lips twisted. Because he did.

Mo hissed and stamped a back foot, but I held his collar. He skulked at my side, his hackles up, his aggression bolstering my courage. A small growl rumbled in his chest as Vujic stepped into the room.

"Hello, Hannah, Avarill. You're both looking well."

Grandma struggled to her feet, her joints stiff after a long day. "Wolfgang Vujic, this is still my residence. You do not waltz in without my permission."

His eyebrows rose, and a sardonic grin grew on his face. "Of course, my apologies. Avarill, you've had time to consider my offer. Will you be coming to work for me?"

"She will not!" Grandma raised her chin with emphasis. "We don't need your dirty money."

My heart spasmed. Apparently, Grandma and I hadn't talked because she'd already decided. I knew what had to be done.

"Grandma, it's okay. What would my hours be?"

Vujic moved closer, his eyes bright with greed. "I am a very fair boss, Ava. May I call you that?"

Ew. My skin crawled. "No, I prefer Avarill."

"Of course," he said. "You'll work five hours a day, with oc-casional late evening hours. I will set up a payment schedule for you. You'll have more than enough to cover the mortgage payments, as well as living expenses. As a precaution, if you are not giving your all to this job, the schedule will become void."

I fisted my hands. "That's illegal. It's blackmail."

"So naïve," he said, just loud enough for me to hear. In a regular voice, he said, "Think of it as an incentive."

"And I won't be working in any of your other businesses?"

Vujic's eyes slid over me again. "If you would rather, I'm sure I could find a place for you. Lillyn is always looking for new girls."

The name of the proprietor of The Nymphhouse, Cristalpeaks' most popular brothel, curdled my stomach.

"If that's your offer, Mr. Vujic, you can leave immediately." Grandma's face turned red and splotchy, and Mo bared his large teeth.

A sour tang coated my tongue. "No. That's non-negotiable."

Vujic didn't seem cowed in the least. "Hmm, pity. Fine. You have my word. You'll be my assistant for a new entertainment arena I've purchased."

Grandma heaved a breath, her hand to her chest as she stepped back. I reached over and took her other hand, giving it a slight squeeze.

She gave me a pained look. Neither of us wanted this, but it was the only avenue. I turned back to Vujic. "When do I start?"

His oily smile widened, which only made my stomach cramp harder. "Tomorrow. Meet me at Fire and Ice Hearth at nine in the morning."

He turned to leave. "Do sleep well, ladies."

Chapter Five

BLAIZ

I WOKE WITH A start, my neck protesting with a shooting pain. Massaging the offending area, I took in my surroundings. I'd fallen asleep in my hoverchair, just like I had the night before.

For the past week, I'd plunged deep into Vujic's systems over and over, trying to find the hole in his protections. One opening was all I needed to crack him wide open, to find the bribes and shady deals hidden in his files. As I expected, the man was tight, his systems as strong as star steel.

Usually, I didn't worry too much about what happened to the marks after I passed along the information. Criminals deserved whatever they got. But I hadn't planned on an innocent like Ava—someone who hadn't done anything wrong and instead had caught Vujic's interest.

I shoved away from my holo desk. Despite all my efforts, Ava would become his employee unless I came up with something soon. Maybe it was already too late, and she'd agreed. My spirit wolf pushed a growl past my lips at the thought of her in trouble. "Me too, pal," I whispered.

If only I hadn't taken Vujic's business... But I had, and now Ava would pay for it.

I stalked to the kitchen and requested a cup of barzina from the Meal Assembly System to clear the fuzziness from my brain. I'd done all I could. Maybe my older brother Bran would have an idea.

After I'd taken a shower and eaten breakfast, I headed down to the ground floor. The gold metallic wanderer gleamed in the low light. It was the newest model, and I'd purchased it as soon as they'd released them to the public. Although the pleasure of a new toy faded within a few weeks, I didn't know what else to do with all my money. So, I sent some to my mom, some to Bran and Blueanne, my sister, and the rest just sat in my account.

The hangar door yawned open as I went through the pre-flight check. While I was thankful I wasn't homeless or on the streets, the money felt dirty. Most of it had been gained from doing businesses with criminals and conmen.

I shook away the thought and headed toward Cristalpeaks. On the Primary Flight Display, brightly lit crosses indicated heavy traffic. I charted a flight through the capital's crowded skies. Low-slung apartment complexes huddled next to the peacekeeping forces' building, while the fire department and a health services facility lay on the opposite side of the city's central square.

My brother's engrafted star steel office building boasted long rock glass windows. Once I parked my wanderer in the visitor's lot, I headed toward the structure. A protective force field stopped me five yards from the entrance. The Kali, a gifted race on Ramilion, had created a unique substance that formed the shimmering barrier. There were very few, if any Kali, in Amaris, but the peacekeeping forces had a contract with the builders. We supplied the schematics, and they supplied the materials and the workers.

I poked at it, and it zapped me with what felt like an electrical shock. I walked toward the five-foot-tall scanner embedded in the dirt at the invisible barricade's edge. Despite the cracked screen, it still worked.

"Name?" the robotic voice asked.

"Blaiz Weylin."

"Please remain still for scanning."

A grid flashed on the screen for several seconds before disappearing. "You may enter."

The force field remained in place, but allowed me through, like squeezing through a heavy, dense liquid. Tingles danced over my skin. Once on the other side, I blinked away the spots dancing in my vision. With a deep breath, I entered the office complex.

Interior white walls, white-tiled floor, and bright hallways shone as if crime wouldn't dare show its face in such brilliance. The faint scent of cleaning solution lingered, and I nodded to the officer at the registration desk.

In his office, my brother slouched at his black desk, the bare walls holding only a flixer of my sister Blueanne, Bran, and me from last summer. The wide window offered a view of the busy streets outside, although it was at my brother's back. While Bran's desk with the inset screen and an office-issued hoverchair dominated the room, a holoscreen half the size of mine at home hung on the wall to his left. A map of Cristalpeaks and the surrounding districts glowed blue and white. A black end table and a matching padded chair occupied a corner.

Bran's brown hair stuck up like he'd run his hands through it. Although we shared the same bone structure, our eyes were different. His were bright blue, just like our mother's. Mine had changed to light brown with the wolf augmentation. *Thanks, Dad.*

I forced the painful memories aside and leaned against his doorjamb. "Hey, Bran. Good morning."

He jerked, his eyes widening. "Hey. I rarely see you around here. Don't stay too long, or we'll put you to work. You know I'm working, right?"

"It's great to see you, too. How's life been treating you?" I walked into the office and dropped into the chair. The lumpy cushion was as hard as a rock.

"Blaiz, I don't have time to visit right now. The supervisor's breathing down my neck about the gang activity in Cristal-peaks."

"I can't help you with that, but I want to help you with a different, persistent problem named Vujic."

Bran's lips twisted. "Yeah, you and every other peacekeeping officer."

A miniature drink assembler stood in the corner, and I requested a barzina. In seconds, I held the hot drink in my hand. "I tried diving into his files, but he's tight."

"What about the invention you were working on a couple of months ago?"

The drink stopped halfway to my lips. I'd completely forgotten about the harvester. "It's in progress. I had to put it aside when my workload increased. I might be able finish it after another night or two."

"Could we use it on Vujic? We'd just need someone to get inside."

"Don't you have an undercover officer for that?"

He leaned back, the dark circles pronounced under his eyes. "He's already being used in another case. Vujic's corporate office is familiar with our other officers, except for Kopanja. He's a rookie, though. Unless you know someone who could get in?"

Shoving a hand in my pocket, I ignored the weightless sensation in my stomach. My father had taught me well—hope was a useless emotion. "Me. Wire me up and get me in."

Bran shook his head. "I doubt my supervisor would go for it. He wasn't happy about you finishing up that job for Vujic."

The one that had caused all the problems for Ava. I took a sip of my drink to hide my expression. "I had to, so he didn't suspect anything when I closed down the business."

"Right. We need someone who he'd never expect. Can you think of anyone like that?"

I took another drink. "Uh, yeah. I can." The animal inside squirmed at the thought of using Ava that way. If it gave her the opportunity to avoid Vujic, though, she'd go for it.

My brother's blue eyes went wide. "Are you kidding me? That's great news. Have him call us."

"Bran, it's Vujic's mark, the last job he wanted information on. He used what I gave him to blackmail her into working for him."

He heaved a heavy sigh. "Hoarfrost. If you give me her name, I can have an officer contact her. We can add her testimony to his file."

"How about a different angle?"

"What do you mean?"

"We're friends. A laced predator attacked her outside my home when she did a delivery. I patched her up. Um, she doesn't know who I am, but she wants to put Vujic away. She might do it."

Bran ran a hand over his face. "You haven't told her about your part in all of it?"

"Are you sunspotted? I'm not sharing that with her. 'Hey, thought you should know I completely screwed up your life, and now you have to work for a crime boss.' No. I'll repair the damage, help her family, and get her out from under his hold. Then I'll tell her." *Maybe. If I have the chance.*

"Do you think that's the best—"

"Do you want me to ask her or not?"

"You don't have to bite my head off, okay?" He considered me, his blue eyes narrowed. "I've never seen you this intense before. Is there something else going on?"

My shadow wolf paced inside, but I ignored him and gave a half shrug. "I just want to fix the problem I created."

"No. Vujic created this." He pursed his lips then nodded once. "If you think she'll help, that would be great. I'll check with my supervisor for clearance."

Our conversation drifted to small talk. I left after he urged me to comm Mom. Never mind the fact I commed Mom every weekend without fail. Bran was solicitous and very protective of her. My father's behavior had affected each member of my family differently. We all survived, but it wasn't until our father died that we felt free.

I flew back to Winter Sun, thinking about what Bran had said. My wolf and the strange guilt I felt over Ava's situation had spurred me forward. While some of my best ideas came when I was under pressure, that hadn't happened this time. I'd frozen when it mattered most. I stilled. Mattered most? When had Ava's problems become so important to me? I shoved aside the questions and spent the rest of the drive thinking about the harvester's design. It needed to work perfectly, with minimal risk to the wearer.

Once I arrived home, I found the half-finished project buried under a stack of paper. It was a handy piece of tech that only needed proximity to work. Bran understood most of what it did, but not how—that was my job. My initial prototype worked, but it was bulky and had a limited range. Harvey 2.0 was smaller and had a range of twelve feet. Anyone carrying this could walk into someone's office, scrape their files, and walk away with all their secrets. Not completely legal, but it was what we needed to demolish Vujic.

I worked on the invention until the buzzing from my BioDock broke my concentration. I checked the screen—my older sister, Blueanne. Arching my back to relieve the ache, I answered the comm, putting it on audio.

"Hi, Blaiz. How are you?"

"Good. How are things on Jesek?" My sister had ended up on that moon to pay off our father's debts. After a disastrous deal, my father was in danger of losing our home. Bran and I had been too young to help, but my father forced Blue to work for his creditor. She surprised us all when the two fell in love and got married. While I missed her, I didn't miss her constant matchmaking attempts, which she tried to do even though she lived far away. That's what being married would do to you—you felt the need to pair everyone else up.

"Fantastic. I'm taking control of the next luxury project on Joya. Can you believe it? A resort on Jesek's sister moon. I have so many ideas. You should come to visit. I'll show you what it'll look like, and I'll give you a deal on a prime location."

"Maybe. What kind of resort is it?"

"Oh, it's solar. We'll be catering to the young professionals, so it'll be the perfect place to relax, socialize, meet that special someone..."

There it was. What all her comms came back to. I rolled my eyes. "I don't want to socialize."

"Blaa-ii-zz," she said, drawing out my name. "That's ridiculous. You just haven't met the right woman yet."

An image of Ava drifted through my mind. Maybe I had met the right one, although I'd ruined it before anything could begin. "I'm just focusing on my career right now."

"You know, I have a friend who's single. She's cute, just relocated to Amaris. I could give her your comm number."

"No. Just no."

"Blaiz, I think you two would hit it off." Blueanne's voice rose with excitement.

My stomach tightened. This would end in disaster unless I put a stop to it. "I already met someone."

Silence pulsed from my sister's end. "You did? When?"

"Just a few days ago. It's early in the relationship, but I really like her." More than it being an excuse, it was true. I liked Ava, her inner strength, the compassion she showed her grandmother, the light that seemed to pour from her soul—

"What's her name? How'd you two meet? Ooh, why don't I invite you two to dinner and you can—"

"Not yet, Blue. It's early days."

She finally agreed to wait, though her excitement drifted over the comm. After a sincere congratulations on her new project, I told her I had to go. She only signed off when I promised to comm her next week with more details.

As I fiddled with the harvester, I reviewed my conversation with Blueanne. I hadn't mentioned Ava's name. After a few weeks, I could tell Blue we'd broken up. Because no solar system existed where our relationship would work. I was the main reason she was working for Vujic.

My spirit wolf growled, unable to understand why I wasn't pursuing her. I pushed a hand through my hair and leaned back in the hoverchair. Because of the augmentation, I was like a laced creature, the foreign DNA twisting with mine to create a phantom lying under my skin. I had amber eyes, alpha behavior, and the need to protect—a wolf with no way to use the skills in the modern world.

The illegal augmentation was my eighteenth birthday present from my father to make me an asset in his business. I'd track enemies, be a vicious killer, and become the CEO when he retired. My father planned to build a criminal empire, like the Sandozi Syndicate, even though they were busted and locked up years ago. While the DNA had given me the skills he'd hoped for, he'd died six months later from a heart attack. Removing an augmentation was a serious risk, and since it was prohibited, I'd face too many questions if I saw a surgeon about it.

It was one good reason among many not to pursue Ava. She didn't need a mutant like me intruding on her life. An interest in her would only hurt us both. Once I extricated her and Grandma Hannah from Vujic and made sure they were safe, I'd step back. Maybe take a trip off-planet, create some distance between the two of us. When Ava discovered who I was, she'd buy my ticket herself.

Chapter Six

Avarill

THE NEXT MORNING, I pulled on a dark brown pair of pants, a warm red sweater, and comfortable yet fashionable brown leather boots. I hoped the outfit was acceptable, since I wasn't sure what I'd be doing. I shrugged. Even though my new boss hadn't given me much of a clue, I guessed I'd be doing something like running errands or making deliveries.

Grandma was up and waiting for me, her dirty breakfast dishes in front of her on the counter. She frowned when I entered. "I'm worried, Ava. Vujic is evil, and working for him will only lead to trouble."

It's not what I wanted either, but I defined trouble as being homeless. The situation seemed impossible, especially after we worked so hard to make things work here. "I'll be fine. He'll probably have me make deliveries, run errands, that sort of thing."

I bolted my breakfast, trying to ignore the worry in her eyes. "He said I would work five hours. That means I'll be home by suppertime, easy."

"If he asks you to do anything dishonest, you leave. This job shouldn't require you to compromise your beliefs."

My smile felt brittle around the edges as I put both of our breakfast dishes in the PureScrub. I wouldn't last long if I followed her advice. I gave her a hug. "Don't worry. See you at supper."

With a final scratch for Mo, I grabbed my red cloak.

Stay. Mo's longing washed over me. "I wish I could, Mo. I really do."

His whine broke my heart as I walked out the door. Outside, the birds were greeting the new morning. They were difficult to connect with. They were usually with their flock, and it created a lot of overlapping emotional noise. I climbed into my wanderer to escape it.

When I arrived at Fire and Ice Hearth, the restaurant was full of breakfasting regulars. I ignored the virtual holomenu of the restaurant specials at the entryway as conversation and the clinking of silverware surrounded me. An Artificial Intelligence synthlife glided through the eating area delivering meals. My mouth watered at the aroma of honey cakes scenting the air. I hoped I wouldn't see Mael. He wouldn't understand why I was meeting Vujic, and I didn't feel like explaining the disastrous events that brought me to this point.

After scanning the room, I found the businessman eating with his associate in a back booth. The man, Vujic's closest minion, was a no-neck thug with thick fingers and dead eyes. I threaded around tables, my jaw clenched so tight my teeth ached. When I reached them, I pulled a chair to the end of the table so I wouldn't have to cozy up with either of them.

"Good morning, Avarill. You're right on time." Vujic gave me one of his classic oily smiles. "I appreciate punctuality."

I don't care what you like. The less I said here, the better. I clasped my hands together under the table.

He continued. "Avarill, meet Kacic, one of my trusted associates."

I forced my face into a neutral expression. "Hello."

The man tossed me a glance and grunted.

"Kacic!"

The minion jerked. "Yes, boss?"

"Greet our newest team member like a civilized man."

"Hi," he said before stuffing a forkful of eggs into his mouth.

Vujic continued. "Allow me to purchase you a barzina while Kacic and I finish our breakfast."

He flagged down a synthlife before I could object. "A barzina for my new employee, please."

She nodded and floated off.

"I don't have any money on me."

"Please." He waved away my concern. "I'm paying. You'll find I'm a very generous employer. I like things a certain way, and I don't mind paying for them to be so."

My scalp prickled. "What exactly does that mean?"

The synthlife returned with my drink, the whipped froth on the top sprinkled with milfoil glow. My nose twitched at its spicy heat before I took a sip.

"It means I expect my employees to be punctual, pleasant, and well-dressed. For example, I'll expect you to wear the company uniform. My orders are exactly that and will not be altered, changed, or disregarded unless I tell you so. Do you under-stand?"

His gaze met mine, his hard eyes suddenly, radiantly blue. The glossy stare pinned me to my chair. My heartbeat galloped, a scream lurking in the back of my throat. With a herculean effort, I nodded, forced my gaze to the table, and took another sip of my drink. The creamy taste of vanilla and spice grounded me.

The moment passed. What the suns was that? I'd never felt like that before—the surety I was facing down a predator and wouldn't make it out of this place alive. With one shaking hand fixed around my mug and the other hidden under the tablecloth,

I focused on my drink while Kacic and Vujic finished eating. After wiping his mouth, Vujic stood and threw a wad of money on the table. "Follow me to headquarters. You can park your vehicle there."

Mael came into view as I was leaving. He stood at the door to the kitchen, his face twisted into a frown. My cheeks burning, I gave him a helpless shrug and trailed the two men to the parking lot. I wasn't thrilled with the situation either, but this was what I had to do.

I followed Vujic's wanderer to Answers Corporation, the suspended office. As I flew closer, my eyes widened. The monstrous triangle of black steel and mirrored windows loomed large. Even rimmed in bright white lights, malevolence seemed to emanate from the monolith, the hangar for incoming traffic a gaping maw.

After parking in the hangar, I exited my vehicle. Vujic met me and gestured toward one of a dozen doorways. Some of them had a company name at the top. Vujic walked toward the door labeled as Suite Forty-seven. "Today is a light duty day. We'll enter your information into the employee database, so you can begin work tomorrow with no delays. I'll show you our offices, then introduce you to Tyffani, our stylist."

"Stylist?"

Vujic gave me a condescending smile. "I have a reputation to uphold, my dear, and my employees' appearance says something about me and my businesses. They, and now you, are a reflection. So yes, you'll meet with my stylist for several sessions today, then come to me for approval. After that, you'll receive your schedule for the week."

My throat thickened. The arrogant tone of his voice opened a chasm between us—the poor and insignificant versus the rich and ruthless. Forcing my embarrassment aside, I focused on thoughts of Grandma and the parents I'd had. I was loved, valuable, regardless of what I wore or how much money was in my pocket. Grandma and I were there for each other through every season, doing what needed to be done. Someone like Vujic would never understand that.

He walked into a hallway fronted by a steel reception desk. As I followed, a whirring sound caught my attention. Tucked into a corner near the ceiling was a camera. In fact, cameras were stationed at regular intervals, sure to track each movement. Shaking away the discomfort of being watched, I turned to face the Artificial Intelligence synthlife manning the desk. Radiantelligence, a multimillion-dollar company based on the planet Ramilion, created most of the AI lifeforms. Customers used them as security personnel, companions, waitstaff, and a dozen other uses. All of them had metallic grids covering their synthetic skin, a giveaway these beautiful beings were AI and not human.

This one had a gold grid covering glowing peachy skin, lustrous red hair, and a uniform that fit her ample curves like it was custom tailored. Her name tag read 5181L. She flashed me a mechanical smile, her bright white teeth gleaming.

Vujic waved his platinum BioDock over the information port, a silver cylinder at the corner of the desk. "Sibil, please create a new employee account with this information. Avarill, I've entered your entry passcode key. Scan to download. You'll use this every time you enter or leave this facility."

This felt like a bad dream, but the scent of Vujic's strong cologne and his intense stare made it all too real. I had the sudden urge to take off running and never stop, to put so much distance between me and Vujic that he'd never find me. But I couldn't leave Grandma. Nausea churned my stomach. Swallowing down the bile, I waved my forearm over the port, and the device beeped, copying the passcode.

Wolfgang Vujic was now my boss.

We moved down the stainless-steel hallway before he turned
to enter a door on the left. With another scan of his BioDock,
the door slid open to a hive of hallways, cubicles, and conference
rooms, all done in sleek metallic finishes, expensive furniture,
and thick carpeting. Glittering, cut crystal lights hovered above
the room, offering illumination where needed. Large golden
urns held ferns and tropical plants impossible to find anywhere
on Amaris. On one wall, an invisible screen displayed a cursive
WVE that appeared than faded. In several corners were small
scanners, watching as employees silently worked at their desks or
hurried off on errands.

Vujic turned to me, a smug smile gracing his wide face as he
strolled down the main hallway. "Welcome to Wolfgang Vujic
Enterprises. I'd give you time to get settled, but you'll need the
extra time with the stylist."

I hid my wince behind a flat expression.

While he punched in a few numbers on his BioDock, I tried
to ignore the curious looks aimed my way from other employees.

"Tyffani," he said into his BioDock, "I have our newest employee with me. Please give her Treatments A through C, then
send her to my office when she's finished."

The tinny voice responded, "Will do, Mr. Vujic."

In seconds, a motorized unmanned chair barreled its way
down the hall. I took a step back, but it stopped directly in front
of me. The chair's glass shield slid up in invitation. I eyed the
molded interior and footrest.

Vujic gestured. "Have a seat. It will deliver you directly to
Tyffani's office suite."

I slid into the leather seat and fastened the attached seat belt as
the shield slid down into place. Next to my right palm, a keypad
waited, filled with buttons and a miniature screen. After finding
a button labeled *go,* I pressed it, and the seat took off down the
hallway.

Although I tried to keep track of the number of left and right turns, the chair moved at a dizzying speed down stainless-steel hallways. It slowed, then stopped before a set of French double doors. Through the clear panes, a spa waited, decorated in cool tones of mint and white. Greenery and exotic plants sprouted from alcoves, and the faint scent of coconut lingered in the air.

I extricated myself from the chair and stumbled into the suite. A brunette pixie with dramatic makeup approached from the back. "Oh, you're here already. You must be Avarill?"

I nodded. "Yes. Are you Tyffani?"

She nodded, her eyes assessing me. Her neon pink eyeshadow glimmered as she squinted. "Hmm, Mr. Vujic asked for Treatments A through C, but it seems a shame to cut that gorgeous hair."

My eyes widening, I put my hands to my hair as if covering it would make it invisible. "Cut it?"

Finally, she shook her head. "No, I can shape it a little but drastically cutting it won't work for you. Let me explain what we'll be doing here. Treatment A is setting you up with uniforms and measuring for your work attire. Treatment B is cutting and shaping your hair, while Treatment C is a full makeover."

My face flamed with heat. I never wore makeup, or bought new clothes, or splurged on an expensive haircut because I didn't have the money. For any of it.

"I can't afford this."

"Oh, hon, don't worry about that. This is all on Mr. Vujic's business account, so no worries." She patted my shoulder. "Many of us come from similar circumstances, but let me tell you—my life changed as soon as I was on Mr. Vujic's payroll."

That's what I was afraid of.

She ushered me into a spacious room. Several mannequins with no faces occupied one corner. Bolts of cream Solknit, melon damask, and bright turquoise shadowool lay tangled on a cutting table. Stacks of red and black uniforms, all sizes, filled the cubbies on one wall. A silky spectralfiber gown embellished with several dramatic splashes of sequins draped a dressmaker's dummy. Rather than using a revealing cut, the design emphasized the mannequin's form.

I pointed it out. "Is that your creation?"

When Tyffani nodded, I smiled. "You're very talented. It's beautiful."

"Thank you. One of these days, I'll open my own shop and design clothes for ambassadors and celebrities."

I hoped she made it out from under Vujic's thumb.

After taking my measurements, she handed me a Solknit shirt and pants and instructed me to try them on in her fitting room. While the clothes weren't low cut, they hugged every curve and roll perfectly. I tugged at the hidden seams, wishing for a looser fit. Why did my newest clothes in years have to be one of Vujic's uniforms?

When I came out, Tyffani looked me over. "I'll keep your measurements on file for any other clothes Vujic might order for you."

Other clothes? A dim feeling of suffocation filled my lungs.

She handed me several sets of uniforms before she took me to the salon area. She washed, trimmed, then styled my hair into beautiful curls. I inhaled the tantalizing scent of coconut.

Smiling, Tyffani handed me a bag. "There's a set of instructions inside to keep your hair looking its best. Remember to use the products. Your hair won't do anything like what we have here without them."

Tyffani guided me to the Treatment C area, a bright white room filled with colorful jars and bottles on one side. On the other wall, a makeup application center waited with its large double-mirrored vanity. I'd seen them advertised but never thought I'd have the chance to use one.

Tyffani waved to the chair in front of it. "Have a seat. Place your chin on the padded frame, and center your face before the concave screen. Remain still, and the center will run a color diagnostic, choose the best makeup for your skin tone, and apply it correctly. It will beep when finished. Don't forget to close your eyes. I think you're smart enough to know that, but the last person tried to keep her eyes open. What an ice cadet." She rolled her eyes.

Sitting in the chair, I leaned forward and placed my face in the hollow area. After closing my eyes, a mist of sweet-scented liquid caressed my face. What followed was a blend of applicators, brushes, and sponges applying various cosmetics to my skin. After a long pause, a faint beep sounded.

I sat back and studied the stranger in the mirror. A foreign sense of poise and the urge to hide blended in my chest. The center had applied my dramatic makeup with impressive precision—smokey winged eyes, pearlescent cheekbones, and glossy pink lips. With my hair curled in beautiful, loose waves and my pristine red and black uniform, I hardly recognized myself. Dropping my head, I took a deep, pained breath. Every month, Grandma and I had just enough to get by, but not much extra. This was a dream—but required by a monster.

I pushed back from the application center and turned to face Tyffani, who waited in the corner. She came closer and wiped a spot from the corner of my eye with a smile. As she placed another sheet of instructions and the makeup products in a bag with the uniforms and hair care products, she said, "Perfect. The new and improved Avarill."

Something forced the words from my throat as I took the bag. "Are you sure about that?"

Her smile wavered. "Let's call your look Extraordinary Avarill instead of Everyday Avarill, okay?"

Emotions swirled in my stomach. The woman reflected in the mirror was polished, confident, strong, molded by Vujic's iron control. How could I like that person?

I forced words past a thick tongue. "Thank you, Tyffani. You did a great job."

She bit her lip before she leaned close. "Look. You seem like a nice girl, and I don't understand why you're here. People like you don't work for Vujic unless there's trouble."

Before I could speak, she held up a hand. "I don't want to know. Just remember, Vujic chews up and spits out nice girls. You need to harden up. This place eats the weak, but if you get stuck, let me know. I might be able to help. After all, you learn things when you've worked in the same place for a while."

My stomach hollowed out at the warning. "Thank you," I said.

Before I could think on it longer, she helped me into the motorized chair with a bag of new products and my old clothes in my lap. I returned via the same route before my ride stopped at an office door. *Mr. Wolfgang Vujic* marched across the door's surface in a bold gold font.

My stomach flipping, I struggled out of the chair. As it backed up and left, I knocked on his door with a trembling hand.

The door slid open, revealing a room with wall-to-wall white carpeting. Expensive art hung on the ivory walls. Vujic sat behind a vast lionwood desk, the inset comm screen casting a faint cobalt glow on his sly smile.

I almost threw up at the hunger gleaming in his expression. "Very nice. I knew there was a delicious female resting underneath those old clothes and unflattering haircut."

Tyffani's words came to mind, and I forced my face into an impassive expression.

Irritation curled Vujic's lips when I didn't respond. He handed me a silver envelope. Next to the embossed WVE on the front glinted a metallic sensor. "Deliver this immediately. Coordinates are already downloaded. Wait for his scan and return the envelope to Sibil. Although you'll be working off-site for the rest of this week, you'll check in here tomorrow at noon, ready to work and receive your coordinates."

With a nod, I left the office as quickly as I could—out of the office, down the hallway, swiping my passkey through the checkpoint, until I was almost running to my wanderer. I jumped into the cockpit and accessed the coordinates.

Setting the autopilot to my delivery point, I settled into the seat as the wanderer left the hangar. While memories of my first day flitted through my mind, a few tears escaped. I allowed my head to fall back onto the headrest. A delivery driver—that's all Vujic needed. That must have been the talents he'd mentioned to Kacic. While I didn't love working for him, I could handle this. It wasn't all that different from my original job. And it would allow me and Grandma to keep the house.

My coordinates delivered me to a rundown area of town on the outskirts of Skift. The address was in a small apartment building with peeling paint and malfunctioning lighting, the low drifting globes snapping and flickering. The narrow stairways smelled of sausages and strong, sour barzina.

After my first knock, a little girl with messy pigtails answered the door. Beyond her lay a small apartment with shabby furnishings.

Her blue eyes narrowed. Despite her young age, she was as suspicious as an old woman.

"Hi." I gave her a smile. "Is your daddy home? A Davud Kordo?"

A thin, pale man appeared behind her. "I've got it, Samira. I'm Davud. Can I help you?"

Stepping back, the little girl crossed her arms with a scowl.

I turned to him and held out the envelope. "I need a scan from you."

His face blanched when he saw the WVE embossed on the envelope. "I'm in the middle of something. I'll do it tomorrow."

I bit my lip and pushed the envelope into his shaking hands. "Um, I need to wait for your scan and return it today."

"Go away," the little girl said. "Leave Daddy alone."

"Samira, shh." He turned back to me. "I just need a little more time. I'll have the last payment by the end of the week."

My heart sinking, I tried to ignore Samira glaring at me and the desperation in her father's eyes. Another of Vujic's victims. "Um, I can't authorize that. I mean, I'm just the courier."

"This-this apartment is all we have."

This small family deserved to be left alone, but since this was my first errand from Vujic, I couldn't fail. "I understand. But I can't return without your scan."

His shoulders drooped. Without a word, he dropped the envelope, grabbed his daughter, and bolted.

Before he could reach the next room, a red laser exploded from the sensor. It paralyzed Davud, who dropped his daughter's hand. The laser grew to a large, red grid until it covered his body. After several seconds, the sensor retracted the red beam, and he dropped to the floor, his muscles twitching.

I took a step back from the sinister silver envelope, but Samira had no fear. She ran over and picked it up before heaving it into the smelly hallway. Tears streamed down her cheeks. "I hate you," she yelled. Before I could offer an apology, she slammed the door in my face.

With two fingers, I picked up the silver envelope and buried it in my bag.

Was Davud Kordo hurt? I loitered in the hallway, torn between escaping and making sure he was okay. When I finally heard a muffled conversation inside, I dashed for the safety of my vehicle.

I flew back to Answers Corporation, my stomach cramping as I replayed the scene in their apartment. Vujic was threatening them, just like he had threatened me and Grandma. How many other people were in similar situations? After handing over the silver envelope to Sibil, I climbed back into my wanderer and flew home.

I engaged the autopilot while questions whirled through my mind. Was I being changed and compromised into a different person? I agreed to work for Vujic, not become someone else. Could I continue to run errands that threatened and scared others? Would I compromise the things I'd stood for my entire life?

The events of the day blended into a depressing, shameful collage—Vujic's predatory expression, Tyffani's warning, the hopelessness in Davud Kordo's expression, and the tears on his daughter's face. I didn't realize I was crying until I parked the wanderer and got out. I leaned my head against its metal side, my tears freezing on my cold cheeks.

"Ava?"

Blaiz stood from his seat on the porch, wrapped in a bronze shadowool coat that brought out the gold tones in his eyes. "What happened?" he bit out as he hurried to my side.

I wiped my face. There was no singular reason for the tears, but the last few hours, along with my questions on the flight home, had left me fragile.

The heat of him radiated through my cloak. "Are you hurt?"

"No, but working for Mr. Vujic isn't as easy as it looks."

"You went to work looking like that?" I couldn't decipher the expression that flashed across his face. Surprise? Dislike? Concern? Maybe it was a mix of all three.

"I didn't have a choice. I went to work, and this is what they transformed me into. This is the standard appearance to work at Vujic Enterprises." Unable to face him, I pulled my full bag of new products from the passenger seat.

"I'm sorry." He shoved his hands in his pockets. "You look nice. I wasn't—"

Ignoring the hollow compliment, I moved to walk past him. "Forget it, Blaiz."

He grasped my arm, his hand warm and his touch gentle. "I'm used to the Ava I met outside my house, not this stranger Vujic expects. Maybe if I'd worked harder, I would've been able to help, prevent you from working for him."

"That's not your job. It is what it is."

"No. It doesn't have to be. I have a plan to shut down Vujic." He leaned closer, looking more alive than I'd ever seen him, his jaw determined. "If you're interested."

The spark in his eyes drew me in, but the memories of the day intruded. Hoping for an escape didn't make one appear. I headed for the side door that led into the kitchen. "How sunspotted is this idea?"

He opened the door for me. "Let's talk about it inside."

Chapter Seven

BLAIZ

As I FOLLOWED HER into the house, I pulled hard on all the conflicting feelings swirling through me. Her situation was my fault, but I wasn't if I could fix this. Why had I come anyway? Sure, I'd visited her grandmother for a while beforehand. But after learning Ava was still at work, I'd waited outside in the cold for her like a love-struck ice cadet.

Ava's silky, white-blonde hair curled over her shoulders, and a form-fitting uniform defined curves I didn't know she had. A layer of makeup hid the sprinkle of freckles across her nose. If I hadn't caught her scent of winter pears, I would've assumed she was an AI synthlife, an artificially enhanced stunner. The natural beauty of the Ava I'd patched up at my house was underneath it all.

Once in the warmth of the cozy kitchen, she tossed her bag on an empty bar stool and greeted Mo, putting her arms around his neck and burying her face in his gray fur. Lucky paszec—I wouldn't mind having her nuzzle my neck in greeting. I stopped, frozen for a moment at the rogue thought. There was no way anything like that would happen. My goal was simple—free Ava and Grandma Hannah from Vujic forever.

Pulling off the lid from a pan of honey cakes, I grabbed two plates from the cabinet.

"Making yourself at home, huh?" she asked with a grin.

I placed two forks on the counter. "Your grandmother told me to feed you when you got home. Have you eaten?"

"I didn't have time. Where's Grandma?"

"She had to run a delivery next door."

Ava looked out the window, her brow furrowed. "I wish she wouldn't do that. It's hard on her joints. Maybe I could do her deliveries when I get home."

"Ava." I touched the warm skin of her wrist, resisting the urge to weave my fingers with hers. "She's made a plan for future deliveries. It's just this one time."

My words didn't seem to register as she slumped onto a kitchen stool. "She'll overdo it and then have to recover in bed for a few days."

"I told her I'll help."

"What?" She looked at me, her mouth falling open a bit.

"I agreed to help her after you leave in the morning, make a few deliveries for her."

"You have your own business. How can you make time for this?"

I'd make all the time in the Duo Soles system for you. The answer lay on my tongue, but I couldn't force the words out. It was the right thing to do, since this whole situation was my fault. "My hours are pretty flexible."

In the past, I'd made so much money with con men, I'd never need to work again. At Bran's urging, I'd gone straight six months ago, but Vujic was a holdover, someone who'd paid in advance. When he contacted me to finish the job, I'd found the information he'd wanted, handed it over, and thrown a party for closing my business to criminals. I vowed to never again take a client that made me feel like I needed a shower afterwards.

"Are you sure about this? I could run the errands when I got home."

"Relax, snowdrop. There's only so many hours in the day, and this is something I can do."

After pouring our drinks, I joined Ava at the counter. After the first bite of honey cake, she licked her lips. "So, what's your plan?"

I took a moment, mentally reviewing the idea my brother and I had mapped out. "The peacekeeping force wants Vujic. If you can get information from his digital files, they could put him away for good."

She leaned forward. "Not to disparage your brother or anything, but the peacekeeping force's efforts haven't been that solar. If it's this easy, why hasn't anyone done this before?"

Rubbing my neck, I refused to look at her. "Nobody could. I'm, uh, really good at breaking into people's systems."

Her brows rose. "Maybe you know the guy that stole my files and gave them to Vujic. His name's Wild. He probably runs in the same professional circles you do."

My muscles tightened. "Probably not. I don't deal with the illegal side of it." At least not anymore.

Ava turned back to her honey cake. "You said *I* have to get his information. How do I do that?"

A feeling of unease wormed through my stomach. "You'll wear a gadget I designed called a harvester. It can pick up a digital signature from up to twelve feet away, crack in, and download the information. The harvester funnels the information to Bran's office in the peacekeeping department. It'll give us the critical information on Vujic and his security, as well as his business dealings."

She bit her lip. "I don't think I'll be able to clear the checkpoint at work wearing it. There are scanners and cameras everywhere."

My muscles loosened. It had made sense to use Ava to get to Vujic. Although I didn't like it, Bran had pitched the idea to his supervisor, who had cleared it. Because Vujic had evaded peacekeeping multiple times, they were willing to try a more daring strategy. But the person who would suffer the most if the plan failed was Ava. "That's fine. We'll think of something else."

Ava pulled off a piece of honey cake and fed it to Mo, before shooting me a thoughtful look. "You know what? Vujic said I'd be working at an off-site work area this week. Maybe I could pick up something there if the security is more relaxed. Would that work?"

The longer we talked, the less I liked this idea. "You don't have to do this."

"Blaiz?"

I flexed my hands. "If there's a computer hookup there, I can access information."

"I'll touch base tomorrow and let you know what I find." Uncertainty dimmed the sparkle in her eyes.

"If you need, we can get some security on the inside."

It was a rash offer. Bran wasn't in charge, and peacekeeping didn't have an infinite number of officers. But my brain kept suggesting all the ways this could flare, all the tactics Vujic would use to hurt Ava if he discovered the harvester.

With a deep breath, she nodded. "Just don't say anything to Grandma about this. She's already worried enough."

After a moment, I asked, "Are your mom and dad around? You and your grandma seem close."

"It's just the two of us. Oh, and Mo." She ruffled the paszec's fur between his ears. "My parents died about three and a half years ago. We originally all lived on a farm on Ramilion, near the Itsavden Empirium. But after Mom and Dad died, we couldn't run the farm on our own."

"I'm sorry they're gone. So, what made a warm-blooded girl like you come here? Amaris is about as different from Ramilion as you can get."

She chuckled. "Do you know I'd never seen snow before I came here? Grandma, though, had visited Amaris often when she was young, so we moved here after selling the farm. What about you? Is your family nearby?"

"As I've mentioned, my older brother, Bran, works on the peacekeeping force. He lives on this side of Cristalpeaks. My mom lives on Amaris's moon, Jesek. She moved there about three years ago to live near my older sister Blueanne, right after I moved out. My dad's dead." I said the last sentence with no emotion, proud of myself for keeping the bitterness out of my voice.

She frowned. "I'm sorry."

"Don't be. He was a lousy father, a worthless husband, and a rotten human being." So much for avoiding bitterness.

Her eyes widened, and the air lay heavy with my words.

"Sorry. I made it awkward," I said.

She shook her head. "No, you were honest. Not everyone gets the father they deserve. You're a great person, despite his shortcomings."

"Thanks." She didn't know me. I'd been skirting around the underside of the law for two and a half years, making money with slimy con men, carbon copies of my dad. I finished my drink. "So, what's Vujic having you do? What are your duties?"

She studied her fork, the tines flashing in the light. "He didn't say. I spent most of the morning bringing my appearance up to code."

"Your appearance? That's hoarfrost, Ava. Vujic shouldn't mess with perfection."

"I—what?"

I hadn't meant to say that last sentence out loud, but the words hung between us. "All these changes," I said, tugging on a long curl, "are unnecessary. It makes you look different, but not better. At least not to me."

Her cheeks flushed.

With a half-smile, I tucked the silky lock behind one ear. "Just something to remember when you have to follow orders."

Wincing, she looked away. "Well, I already had to follow one of his orders. He had me run a delivery, but I survived. If that's all I'm doing for Vujic, it's a relief. I expected worse."

"Like what?"

Frowning, she poked at the dessert in front of her, her shoulders hunched. She bit her lip and turned to look at me. "If I tell you, it's going to sound sunspotted."

"I can do sunspotted."

Silence filled the air. I could almost see her wrestle with her words. Is this where she would tell me her secret? Even though I already knew it, I wanted to hear it from her. *Because it will make you feel less guilty.* I shoved the troublesome voice down deep. "Avarill?"

Glancing over at me, her eyes widened. My spirit wolf pushed forward under my skin, certain dominance was the answer. My eyes were probably glowing as gold as my metallic wanderer. *Not now. Don't force her.* I sat back.

She blinked once then seemed to shake her head. "I thought Vujic would want me because of a gift I have. It's a very personal issue, and it can't become public knowledge."

I nodded, unable to speak past the lump jammed in my throat.

"I had a brain tumor removed ten years ago. Although the surgery was successful, I soon discovered an ability I didn't have before. I could connect with animals."

"Without an augmentation?" I asked. The law permitted only adults to get those, but that didn't mean children never received augmentations. I was Exhibit A. Many things were possible with enough money and connections.

"Yeah. The medical services theorized the stardust energy used for healing during the surgery was tainted. Since I was otherwise healthy, my family chose not to sue the surgeon. In return, they buried all reports of my new ability."

The files I'd found hadn't given details. A procedure with tainted stardust energy could've ended in tragedy. "You're lucky you weren't hurt."

"I know. Even with the energy augmentations and medical advancements, brain surgery is still a delicate operation."

"So, when you say connect... Do you mean you can talk to animals, and they talk back?"

"No. I feel their emotions, and sometimes, I can affect them with my response."

I raised a brow. "You can feel when they're happy? Scared? Sad?"

"Right. I'm what they call a fauna empath."

"Yet, the other night, that laced creature still attacked you."

She frowned. "It was angry, confused, hungry. To be honest, its feelings were all over. I couldn't get a clear read on it."

"Being an empath isn't much good if you can't protect yourself."

She shot me a glare. "It's different with a laced creature. And being an empath means emotions can go both ways. I felt all its emotions plus my own. Sometimes, it makes me dizzy, or I get a headache."

"You're affected like that every time?"

"Only when it's an intense situation. It hasn't happened often, so it's easy to keep the ability to myself. My parents did what they could to hide it. They didn't want anyone to discover what I could do."

Kids were lousy at keeping secrets. "Was that difficult to do?"

"It was at first. But about a year after the surgery, a research scientist stopped at the farm. He worked for the R&D sector of the government and had heard rumors from a hospital nurse. My parents deflected most of his pointed questions. When he could see he wasn't getting anywhere, he brought out a rabbit he had in the back of his wanderer."

My stomach pitched, not liking where this was going.

"He let me pet it, put it back in its cage, and then tortured it to see my reaction. I felt its confusion, the panic and terror, all of it almost like a physical pain."

Anger roared forth, but I fisted my hands, bottling the fiery rage. I wanted to strangle the scientific quarkhead, but he was long gone, leaving Ava with only a terrible memory.

She dashed away a few tears. "It was one of the worst days of my life. My father convinced him I was a normal kid who didn't like to see animals in pain. Thankfully, we never saw him again, and my parents paid a man to destroy my medical records."

"I'm so sorry, Ava." The words felt small, useless.

She nodded then pushed her dessert aside.

I left soon after, my mind full of everything she had shared. She needed down time after work, and I needed to put distance between us. I was getting to where I *needed* to see Ava. Not good, since this relationship couldn't go anywhere.

On my way home, I thought more about Ava and her grandmother's situation. Why was I so eager to help her and her small family? Maybe it was Ava's strength and her love for her grandmother. The light emanating from her made me want to bask in her presence, like a patch of warm sun on a chilly day. I rolled my eyes at my whimsical thoughts. My inner wolf was driving me inside, intent on righting this wrong, to bring about a better ending for Ava. Never mind the fact he was sunspotted about her.

I couldn't forget the look on her face the night Vujic had shown up. I'd been about to return to the living room to say goodbye to Ava, but hearing his voice had stopped me in my tracks. Although we'd never met face to face, I couldn't let him discover a connection between me and Ava. Instead, I'd spied on the scene from behind the kitchen door. Vujic had looked at Ava like a shiny new toy, and my wolf had wanted to rage into the room and challenge him. I'd retreated to the area behind the glass house until he'd flown away in his wanderer. As penance, I'd spent the next two days trying to discover a way to remove Ava and Grandma Hannah from Vujic's greedy grasp.

After parking my wanderer, I opened my BioDock and commed Bran. "Hey. I just came back from Ava's place."

"Ava, huh? You're on a first name basis. Interesting."

"Shut up, Bran. She says there are too many scanners in the main office, but Vujic mentioned she'll be at an off-site work station. She said she'll see if security is just as tight there."

"Since we're using a civilian, we'll need to put the rookie in there for backup. She won't know he's there, but it'll keep her safe. If your girl comes through for us, we might finally nail this guy," Bran said.

Before entering my house, I scanned the backyard. I'd felt less safe ever since Ava's encounter with the laced creature. "She's not my girl."

Bran chuckled. "Right. At least not yet."

Not ever, when she learned what I'd done.

After a few more minutes of small talk, I shut off the comm and headed to my kitchen. I requested a cup of barzina from the Meal Assembly System, then sprinkled some milfoil glow across the whipped cream top.

A couple of clients still needed me to finish up their requests. I'd be done by supper time and then what? Catch the newsfeeds, read, *visit Ava.*

I groaned. That small voice was the same as the wolf within me. I was thinking about her more than I should, wondering what she was doing, worrying if she was okay. Once she learned the truth, though, she'd want nothing to do with me. I couldn't forget that. I'd be a lone wolf, like nature intended.

Chapter Eight

AVARILL

I REPORTED TO VUJIC in his office at noon as instructed. My hair still held the curls, but since I didn't have a makeup application center, getting ready took a half hour longer than I expected. It was a minor miracle I looked as pulled together as I did.

Vujic took his time looking me over, my skin crawling as he did so. "Today, you'll be meeting my associate, Andrija. He's the manager at Lodestar, my new entertainment facility."

I nodded, although unease threaded through me. Everything about Vujic made me nervous.

"You'll be working there for the next three days, twelve to eight. On Friday and Saturday, you'll work there for an evening shift. Six to two."

"In the morning?" When he had mentioned late evenings, I thought he meant ten or eleven, not early morning.

"Yes. Is that a problem?" he asked, but his tone said it better not be.

"Of course not, Mr. Vujic. Just clarifying."

"Please, call me Wolfgang. We don't need to stand on formality."

I clenched my jaw. Only my second day, and he was testing the boundaries. "I shouldn't. After all, you're my employer. Is there anything else?"

His eyes hardened. "No," he bit out. "See Sibil on your way out. She'll download the coordinates of your worksite for you."

I left his office. As promised, the synthlife gave me what I needed before I left, and once in my wanderer, I loaded the information into the Mapifest Register.

The map came up on the screen. Lodestar was on The Borders, the boundary between the districts and Cristalpeaks. I'd been out there last week when I had desperately extended my hours. It was mostly apartment buildings, although the commercial sector was growing.

As I flew toward my worksite, I passed a floating billboard stating Lodestar as *The Place to Be*. The backdrop of dark mountains offset the spotlights in the foreground. While dramatic silhouettes of a curvy female and muscled male were the focus, the lone piece of information listed was a comm number to purchase tickets.

I located public parking on a nearby rooftop and landed the wanderer. At street level, I threaded past pedestrians on their lunch breaks and found the building without trouble. It was a multi-story columned monstrosity lined with lights and mirrored glass. Illuminated strobing graphics like fireworks surrounded the sign reading *Lodestar*.

Hmm, subtle.

Inside, the lobby layout funneled visitors to half a dozen clear booths protected by rock glass and silver mesh screens. Only one was occupied. The heavily made-up brunette attendant watched me approach and crossed her legs, showing them off in the short skirt and high heels. "We're not open now," she said in a bored tone.

"I know. I'm here to meet Andrija. He's expecting me."

One dark sculpted eyebrow rose, but she didn't move.

What did she want from me? I stifled my irritation. "I'm the new assistant, Avarill Engle. Vujic sent me."

She pursed her lips. From under the counter, she pulled out a silver handheld scanner. "Passcode key?"

I held out my forearm, and she scanned my BioDock. The suspicious pucker of her crimson lips disappeared. "Through the double doors at the end of the hall. I'll let him know you're here."

"Thanks." I headed toward the doors, not sure what I'd find on the other side. Maybe a casino? Racetrack? A holo game arcade? Since I was making deliveries, it didn't matter too much.

Luxury waited past the last booth—gold-veined marble floors, mirrored walls with gilt trim, and a full-length bar on each side of the room made of dark, polished wood.

Biting my lip, I cracked open the double doors to a large arena. Purple swaths of thin, glistening material draped from the center of the vaulted ceiling to the upper level of seating. Each seating level held row upon row of seats, cascading down to a raised platform surrounded by a perfectly transparent rock glass shield. Four tunnel openings, one on each side, opened toward the platform. More purple material and glittering white lights rimmed the tunnel openings.

Two men stood on the platform below, throwing practice punches at each other. Although I wasn't a fighting expert, I could tell there wasn't much force behind the punches, just a lot of ducking and weaving until they made contact. Since they were the only people there, maybe they would know where Andrija was.

As I made my way down the stairs, I trailed a finger over a VIP seat. Upholstered in crushed purple velvet, the seat had temperature and massage controls. Vujic had thought of everything.

I reached the bottom where the two men still feinted and threw punches until one caught sight of me. He paused. "Are you Avarill?"

"Yes, I'm looking for Andrija."

"Well, you've found him." He tossed a towel to his shirtless, muscle-bound partner. "Hydrate, then head for the gym."

The mountain of a man nodded and then left the cage, his muscles rippling as he blotted his neck.

Andrija pressed a button on his BioDock. The shield rose with a whisper, and he joined me beyond the platform. His eyes, a peculiar shade of bluish brown, missed nothing. He gave an appreciative nod. "Vujic was right. You're a pretty thing. You'll fit in fine."

My back stiffened. "Excuse me?"

His brows rose. "What? You think our customers want to see an old, dumpy assistant?"

I glared. What did my appearance or age have to do with making deliveries?

Andrija ran a towel through his salt and pepper hair before looping the towel around his neck. "He does this all the time. Vujic didn't tell you anything, did he?"

When I shook my head, he sighed. "Come to my office. I'll give you the rundown."

A rundown on deliveries? It made sense. Vujic was a perfectionist, with specific preferences. Despite my mental reassurance, my stomach pitched. I pulled in a couple of deep breaths.

We exited the arena via one of the tunnels. The hallway split, one side a track that herded customers back into the arena, the other leading to a gate. Andrija unlocked the gate with his fingerprint then proceeded down a cinder-block hallway. No opulence here—perhaps Vujic had finally run out of money. Andrija opened an ordinary steel door labeled *Manager* and ushered me inside.

For the hundredth time, I tried optimism. There was nothing to be worried about, just a normal delivery post, but I couldn't convince myself. This was Vujic's operation—of course, it wasn't a simple job position.

The cluttered room held a table and two hoverchairs. A battered filing cabinet sat in one corner. A floating shelf displayed several trophies and flixers of previous winners. The sweaty, and sometimes bloody, guys smiled through their mouth guards, raising and shaking clasped arms over their heads.

As Andrija sat behind the desk, I hopped into the hoverchair on the other side, my feet dangling. I pushed a button to lower the seat until my toes brushed the floor.

"This seems to be a surprise for you. Let me explain the job requirements." He gestured to my clenched hands. "It's not as nefarious as you might be thinking."

Then why hadn't Vujic explained anything? "Please enlighten me."

Andrija's lips quirked. "Right. So, Lodestar is a cage fighting arena. We'll be hosting regular cage fights, as well as weaponized and animal cage fights."

Cage fighting? I raised my eyebrows.

"Regular cage fights are man versus man. The weaponized cage fights are armed man versus armed man. No guns permitted. We erect a triple rock glass shield to protect the audience. The animal cage fights are a fresh addition. The fighters sign up, and we'll provide an apex predator—you know, a tiger or lion. We hired a veterinarian and an animal behaviorist besides the usual trainers, physicians, and therapists. One of the open positions is a cage girl. That's your position."

So, no deliveries. I found my voice buried under a thick layer of anxiety. "What does a cage girl do?"

Andrija shifted in his chair. "You usher the fighter of our house to the cage, make sure he has water, a clean towel, get the physician if his trainer asks for it. Then you stand there, cheer for him, and look pretty. After the fight, you leave the platform with the trainer and the house fighter, go back to your dressing room, and you're done. It's a pretty straightforward job."

None of this made sense. Why did Vujic hire me as a cage girl? Because he could. It was another way for him to control me, to manipulate me into doing whatever he wanted. "What about the predator he fights? Do I offer it a towel, too?"

Andrija chuckled. "No, you'll help the trainer get the animal to the cage platform, and we'll give you a tranq gun in case the predator gets loose. It's unlikely, but safety first, you know. We don't expect the guys to win against an apex predator."

My mouth fell open. "You're going to let an audience watch a man be eaten alive?"

"No, we won't let it go that far, although I expect the fighters will be pretty bloody by the time it's all over. You'll be there for the audience to focus on if they get squeamish. There's a lot of money to be made in this, both for us and the fighters. You're lucky to be a part of it. Once the arena becomes established, you'll have a nice hefty salary."

Which I'd need to pay off the mortgage. My cheeks heated, anger and nerves flooding through me. At least Vujic wouldn't be asking me to use my talent. Of course, I'd be able to sense what the animal was going through, but I'd have to focus on something else and try to ignore the emotions flooding me.

The control Vujic held over me cinched tighter. Blaiz's idea about the harvester would be the perfect solution. Now that I knew what was happening here, I wanted to close this place down soon.

"Are these fights legal?"

The man nodded. "Yeah, most of them."

Most of them. This is the point where Grandma would've wanted me to pack up my things and say thanks, but no thanks.

But I couldn't leave, not yet. "How much security is available during the other fights? Will I be at risk?"

Andrija eyed me. "When the assistant is out near the crowd, we have a bouncer assigned to her. We remove any drunk and disorderly patron that gets too bold." He paused. "Any more questions?"

So many thoughts swirled through my mind, but I needed time to process. "Not right now."

"Great. Let me introduce you to Shelah, the assistant you'll be replacing."

"I thought this was a new business."

Andrija punched in a comm number on his BioDock. "Vujic has always held these fights, but he's making it official with this new building. Shelah has been with us for a long time, but she's pregnant and getting chunky."

"There's so much wrong with that comment."

Andrija shrugged. "It's a cut-throat business."

The manager seemed like an okay guy, just not as progressive in his view of women as I would've liked.

Shelah arrived minutes later. The dirty blonde was of average height, with a baby bump, glittering hazel eyes, and a mischievous smile.

She held out her hand. "Nice to meet you. I'll be training you this next week. Don't worry—this job is easy."

As I shook her hand, I pushed my shoulders back. I could do this, especially if I didn't have to see Vujic too much. It wasn't ideal, but I could do it.

For the next hour, Shelah showed me my dressing room, complete with a makeup application center, and went through her pre- and post-fight schedule. Afterwards, she showed me the offices. I perked up at the end of our tour.

"Vujic's office," she said, gesturing to the closed door as we passed. "He hardly ever uses it, although I've heard he watches the fights in there via live camera feeds. Oh, and he also meets with the investors and other businessmen in there, too. Other than that, he's never here."

If he met with investors there, it was likely a proper office with a computer desk. There weren't any visible scanners or cameras. All I needed was a digital connection for Blaiz's harvester to work.

Andrija found Shelah and me in the arena cafeteria having supper. "Avarill, a message came in for you. Vujic wants you to head back to headquarters to meet with Tyffani."

I tried to ignore the heaviness in my chest as I got up to leave.

Shelah gave me a grin. "Tomorrow, we'll go through a rehearsal. After all, the first match is Friday."

As I drove back to Answers Corporation, questions about the upcoming brawl filled me. What kind of fight was it? Did I have the stomach to watch two men pummel each other? How would I handle the predator fights? Memories of the tortured rabbit rose. I shook my head. I had no other option.

My stomach was in knots by the time I parked in Answers Corporation's hangar.

Tyffani met me in the main offices, her green eyes vivid from her glittery orange eyeshadow. "I figured you'd have trouble finding my suite, so I'll escort you. Pop quiz tomorrow," she said with a smile.

Today, her suite smelled like citrus instead of coconut. She led me into the dressing room. "Okay, so Vujic ordered two outfits for you, one for each fight night."

"Oh, I won't wear my uniform?"

Tyffani's brow furrowed. "No, he's looking for something with more drama."

My shoulders slumped as she pulled up the design. A hologram hung mid-air, the faceless model draped in a clinging

Solknit jumpsuit with several cutouts on the sides and a plung-
ing neckline.

I scowled at the design. I'd worn more fabric in the scorching
desert climate of Ramilion. "Really? Maybe I'm being too mod-
est, but I'd like to keep the important areas covered up."

Biting her lip, Tyffani sketched in a few extra lines. "I can put
illusion mesh panels in there to give you more coverage. Maybe
a few other additions."

The alterations would make a difference. I offered her a smile.
"Thank you."

She closed out the design before opening a new one. "And this
one is for the Saturday night fight."

As I took in the red glitter and tiny straps, my mouth dropped
open. "That's—that's a sequined bikini. I can't wear that."

Tyffani gave me a sympathetic look. "Vujic's instructions. He
was very clear on what he wanted for Saturday."

"Did he make Shelah wear this kind of thing?"

"Sometimes, for major fights." She bit her lip. "Look, I'll sew
a cape you can wear with it. Maybe some sheer sleeves. After all,
it can get cold in the arena."

If I could get enough incriminating information on Vujic, I'd
wear the costume. It wouldn't be forever, but I didn't want Tyffani to be punished. "Will you get in trouble for the changes?"

She gave me a secretive smile. "Designer's prerogative. I'll try
to have these finished the day before, but if they're not, I'll send
them via courier. They'll be ready."

"Thanks."

On my flight home, my mind combed through every hallway
and room I'd seen. If there were hidden scanners or cameras,
I'd be in trouble. With a frown, I straightened my shoulders.
Our plan was in place, and there was no room for worry or
second-guessing.

Chapter Nine

BLAIZ

IT WAS TIME TO admit it—I was pathetic. I couldn't help myself. Ava drew me unlike any other woman I knew. Grandma Hannah appreciated the errands I ran for her, even though I hung around afterwards. The quirk of her lips told me she knew why I was waiting.

Last night, I'd finished fine-tuning the harvester for Ava. In my worry, I'd added a safety feature. If the harvester detected a security system, it would emit a vibration against her skin and turn off. This device was the fastest way to take down Vujic, but if Ava's workplace was too secure, we'd have to find another way to catch him. While he could be arrested for extortion, Bran and his captain were hoping for more. Damning information from his files would be critical evidence to keep Vujic and his associates jailed for a long time.

After finishing a few deliveries for Grandma Hannah, I headed for the kitchen where a cobbler cooled on the kitchen counter. She'd promised me a piece. My mouth watered as the scents of dazzleberry jam and rich honey mingled in the air.

The front door opened before I could get out a plate. Ava peeked around the kitchen doorway, and my heart jumped.

"Hi," she said with a tired smile. "I hoped you'd be here. Where's Grandma?"

Euphoria spiraled through me. The warmth in her expression had my fingers aching to touch her. "She's reading in her bedroom."

"You didn't have to stay."

I wanted to see you. I forced a shrug. "Someone has to feed you. How was work?"

The happiness drained from her face. "Well, I figured out my job description."

"I thought you were doing deliveries."

Her cheeks flushing, she grabbed two glasses from the cabinet. "No. I'm the new cage girl at Lodestar, the latest fight arena out on The Borders. Vujic is taking his fights public. I get to introduce the house fighter and assist him from outside the cage during the fight."

In the past, I'd been to a fight or two. My heart pounded at the thought of Ava in revealing clothes. As I imagined other guys checking her out, a growl rumbled from my chest. I turned it into a cough and fisted my hands. Most of the fight clubs drew men like Vujic and my father. And I was the one who put Ava there. Grimacing, I pulled at my collar. "That's rough. I'm sorry."

"Yeah. Me, too. The good news is I think I can take the harvester in. It'll have to be tomorrow or the next day because on Friday and Saturday, my costumes are, ah, different. Is it ready?"

I pulled the device from my pocket. "Here. Put it some place you won't lose it."

She took the disc, the size of a small coin. "It's so light. Thank you. Knowing you and Grandma Hannah are behind me helps."

"Of course." That was me, just a supportive friend, though I wanted so much more. "Ava, are you sure it's safe?" *Say no, I'll think of something else.*

Her smile was without mirth as she poured two glasses of milk for us. "Sure? No, but I'm not working for him any longer than I have to."

I grasped her hands, her fingers delicate yet strong in mine. "Ava, Vujic won't just fire you if he discovers the harvester. Nobody crosses him."

"And if we don't try, I'll have to work for him until the mortgage is paid off. Then he'll find another way to control me. He won't stop." She shuddered. "I can't give up. Let me take a chance."

Just because I understood her desire didn't mean I wanted her to do it. With every minute that passed, the more convinced I was our plan was doomed. Still, all I said was, "Have a seat at the counter."

Sliding onto a bar stool, she watched me plate up two servings of cobbler. I placed a serving in front of her and joined her. "You could hide the harvester in a pocket, sew it into a cuff. I even added a security detector. If it finds a scanner or a camera, it will emit a vibration and immediately turn off."

She nodded. As she took the bite of her cobbler, she closed her eyes in bliss. I sat there, my fork suspended. If I kissed her, would that expression fill her face? She'd taste like fresh berries, rich honey, and a tantalizing flavor that would be completely Ava. The sudden urge to lean in and cover her lips with mine swept over me, but I stabbed a piece of the cobbler and shoved it in my mouth. It was a poor substitute for a kiss.

After several bites, she spoke without looking at me. "I feel horrible."

"Are you sick?" I shot a quick look at her, noting her flushed cheeks and tired eyes.

"No, I mean, being exposed to Vujic every day. Almost like he's trying to wear me down. At this point, nothing he did would shock me. And you know what the worst part is?"

I shook my head, my dessert forgotten in the face of her vulnerability.

Tears welled in her eyes, and her voice grew choked. "Despite all of it, deep down, I liked the haircut, the makeover, the new clothes, although I didn't want to. Knowing I won't have to ask Grandma for money or work extra hours just to buy lip gloss is a relief. So, what does that say about me? Does that make me a monster like him?"

"No, Ava." The pain in her voice ripped into me, and I captured her hand. It fit mine perfectly, like we'd done this a thousand times before. "It makes you honest. You're still the same person inside, where it matters. No matter what your hair looks like or how much makeup you have on, you're still you with the same values and love inside."

"I feel like he's trying to change me into something I'm not, and a small part of me is wondering if he's going to use it for leverage. 'Look at everything I've done for you,'" she said in a poor imitation of Vujic.

A tear escaped and slid down her cheek. "He's got everything he could ever want. Yet Grandma's one of the most wonderful people you'll ever meet, and she has to struggle just to keep her house."

To Vujic, controlling Ava was just another way to assert dominance. The sooner we could close him down, the better. I never imagined he'd use the information I'd gathered like this. My throat thick, I brushed away the tear lingering on her cheek. "We're going to fix this. We'll be working together to put him away, okay? You're not doing this alone, Ava. I'm right here."

As her gaze met mine, her mouth parted slightly. The wolf inside me surged forward, but I forced him down. Since he was driven by instinct, I couldn't follow his lead. He shouldn't even be inside me.

"Your eyes," she said, her voice quiet. "They're gold."

I couldn't hold her gaze. "Sorry. I have an unusual augmentation, courtesy of dear ol' dad. Wolf DNA."

"Wolf DNA? That's—suns, that's really solar, even if it was
from your father. What does it do?"

"You mean besides making me an animal? Aggression. Tracking. Being a leader, which usually translates to being the most
arrogant ice cadet in a room."

She touched my forearm. "I've never considered you an animal, Blaiz."

Her words hung between us. The heat from her hand spread
from my arm through my chest, and her face tilted up towards
mine. The urge to kiss her hit again.

Ava licked her lips, and I swallowed a groan. Was that an invitation? It looked like one. But if I made a move because I'd read
this situation wrong, I'd lose so much more than my pride. The
brief thought of her pushing me away made it hard to breathe. I
shifted my attention to my dessert.

Despite her invitation to stay longer, Ava kept yawning, so I
left after my serving of cobbler was gone. At home, I pulled up
my bank account on my BioDock. The idea had come together
in Ava's kitchen and had only grown since.

Working the underbelly of Cristalpeaks' businesses had filled
my account with more puli than I could ever spend in this lifetime. I had plenty of toys—the newest metallic hovercar parked
in the basement, a top-tier security system, a vacation home
on the planet of Isvora. What if I used my money to help her
instead?

Making a general assumption, I ran a few numbers of how
much I thought their house was worth. Even if it was on the high
end, I could offer Ava and her grandmother enough to pay off
the mortgage.

The whole idea smacked of charity. It was, but only because I
needed to keep them safe. While running errands for Grandma

Hannah, I'd gotten to know her more and learned she was a proud woman and might not take a handout. Even if she did it to protect her granddaughter, Vujic would find another way to get what he wanted. He'd continue to make his illegal deals unless Bran found another infiltrator to bring the man down.

So why was I doing this? Was it guilt because of my part in her problem? Or was my motivation something deeper, something that looked a lot like love?

I snorted, the sound like a gunshot in the quiet room. This was ridiculous. Why would she fall for a mutant freak with wolf DNA? While being only friends was painful, it was better than nothing. I should've kept my distance, but it became impossible. Her radiant smile and sweet heart drew me in. A weak tendril of hope poked through. Maybe, if this plan to destroy Vujic worked, I could see if there was a possibility of a relationship between us.

I scrubbed a hand down my face and stared at my bank account, the numbers growing blurry before I shut down the BioDock. I'd need a grand gesture to offset the damage I'd done, but money was no object. All that mattered was Ava.

Love. The one thing I never allowed myself to consider, not with my animal so close to the surface. In dangerous or emotional situations, my eyes would turn gold as the predator took over. The person on the receiving end would look away in submission. I never wanted to use that on Ava. Instead, I wanted her to want me of her own free will, to accept the animal under my skin.

Slumping back in my hoverchair, I imagined a life I'd never dared to hope for—the two of us together, Ava making her daily deliveries while I worked until she came home. Or we could spend our time visiting Ramilion or my vacation home. We could spend lazy days exploring together and our nights... Groaning, I forced away the thoughts. All fantasy.

Still, the idea of freeing Ava and her grandmother from Vujic's hold wouldn't go away. Before I lost my nerve or overthought it, I commed Ava.

"Hey, Ava."

"Blaiz, hi. Didn't I just see you?" she said, a smile in her voice.

"Uh, yeah. Ha ha," I choked out a strained laugh. "I had a sunspotted idea."

"I can do sunspotted," she said, parroting my earlier words.

"Right." I wiped my clammy hands on my pants. "So, I've never mentioned it, but I have some money saved. What if I bought a new place for you and your grandmother? You could leave Vujic far behind. He'd never bother you two again."

The quiet hum of my server sounded like a cargo carrier engine.

"Are you serious?"

My wolf leaped inside, thrilled she was considering it. "Yes, it's—"

"Why?" she asked. "That's your money, and houses aren't cheap."

Because I'm sunspotted about you. "I told you, I have more than enough. I'd like to give it to you—a gift—so you can get away from Vujic."

"We don't need your pity, Blaiz," she snapped.

"No," I rushed the answer. "That's not what this is. Our plan is dangerous, and it could go wrong in a dozen ways. A safer solution would be to move to a new house far away."

"But the harvester, your invention, could bring Vujic down. Then we wouldn't need to move."

I couldn't contain the small growl that ripped from my throat. "It's not foolproof. Anyone who wears it puts themselves at risk."

"Don't you think that's my decision to make?"

Game over. I dropped my head. "I'm trying to keep you and your grandmother safe."

Her voice softened. "We appreciate it. But this is something I need to do. If we move somewhere else, he wins. He'll continue to run his dirty businesses and intimidate other innocent people. I want to put him away, so he never hurts anyone again."

"Okay. I understand." My wolf, who had been celebrating, huffed once and left to pout in a far corner of my consciousness.

After thanking me, Ava signed off. I wilted, my failed plan lying in tatters around me. Vujic still had to be taken down, one step at a time. Which meant I needed to put into place the next piece of the plan. I commed Vujic, using text only.

Have discovered more information on the initial contact. Are you interested? Contact me for payment and details. Wild.

I clenched my jaw so hard, pain crawled toward my temples. Even though my offer was only a lure, the familiar slime of a dirty deal coated my heart. Why had I allowed myself to get involved in the criminal side of this business?

An hour later, my BioDock buzzed with an incoming message. *I thought the report on the contact was complete. Send whatever you have with the new invoice. I want data on the guardian's financials and medical issues, as well.*

I'll assume this was a simple oversight. It would be a shame for your family to suffer for your incompetence. I trust we understand each other.

As I read the implied threats, my vision clouded with a red haze. Nothing good would come from him knowing more about Grandma Hannah, but I had to follow through to make everything look legitimate. I added an extra fee to the one already settled for Ava's fake information and entered the amount in my BioDock. As soon as I sent the invoice, I called Bran.

When he answered, the words spilled out through my tight jaw. "Vujic took the bait, but he asked for more specifics on Ava's grandmother, financials and medical. He also insinuated the family could be in danger, which means he's probably digging into all of us. You, Mom, and Blue have to be careful. I need damage control, Bran."

"Okay, don't get your shadowool wet. I'll have a member of the force create a fake dossier and send a detail to watch their house. I have a colleague on Jesek that can monitor Mom and Blue for a short time." He paused. "There's a little wrinkle in our former plan."

My stomach plunged. "What?"

"The plant has the flu."

"Flu? He doesn't have the health enhancement?"

Bran sighed. "He can't afford it, and the force doesn't give us a discount on them."

Ava couldn't be in there alone without backup. "Use a physipad on him and give him pain relief. He'll be fine."

"He's vomiting and has a fever of a hundred and two, Blaiz. It's not happening. No worries, though. We've got a replacement."

"Great. Who?"

"You."

"Me?" I waited, expecting to hear him laugh at the joke. In my living room, the cozy fire popped behind the grate, the small sound an explosion in the silence. "I have no clue how to go in undercover."

"You go in as yourself. Hopefully, Ava will get us information tomorrow or Friday. On Friday night, you go to the fight and hand deliver the fake report to Vujic. We won't be far behind you, and we'll bust him while you're there."

I frowned. "You'll have to take me in, though, to make it look like a true raid."

"Right. We'll release you later."

"Hoarfrost, Bran, I hate the idea. If it's all you've got..." I let the sentence hang.

"Come on, Blaizer. The supervisor gave it a gold star. I know you can do it."

I rolled my eyes. "If you're using that old nickname, I know we're in trouble."

Bran chuckled. "It'll be fine. And we'll finally have Vujic."

He couldn't disguise the anticipation in his voice. There was an answering tug, deep in my chest.

After we signed off, I pressed my lips together and leaned back in my hoverchair. This set-up had to work. I'd hand over the information in Vujic's office with Ava none the wiser. Then Wild could disappear forever. Once Bran had Vujic locked away, there'd be a chance for Ava and me.

Chapter Ten

AVARILL

ON THURSDAY, I'D DEBATED where to place the harvester but finally slid it in the bottom of my shoe. With a silent prayer, I headed for the entrance to Lodestar.

Tugging on the heavy door, I slipped inside. Again, the lone brunette from yesterday waited in the last booth. Could she tell I was wearing the harvester? My stride felt off, but rather than obsessing, I offered her a friendly smile. When our gazes met, she glared. My smile faltering, I looked away. *Just head for your dressing room, Ava.*

"Hold it right there," the brunette said as she stood.

My heartbeat pounded in my ears. "Yes?"

She held up her index finger and twirled it in the air. "Do one turn, slowly."

I knew it. A hidden camera must have tipped her off. I checked the corners of the lobby. There was no sign of a scanner, and I hadn't felt a vibration from the harvester. I obeyed her instruction as my limbs tingled.

She folded her arms. "Who did your hair?"

"My—what?"

With narrowed eyes, she pointed to my head. "Your hair. My hairdresser quit yesterday."

I released a quiet, yet shaky breath. "Uh, Mr. Vujic's stylist. Her name is Tyffani."

Scowling, her shoulders slumped. "Oh. Thanks anyway."

The rush of relief followed me to my dressing room, where I stored my coat and bag with shaking hands. After meeting with Shelah, the hours passed with no opportunities to linger near Vujic's office. Shelah spent the day describing everything—her skincare products, her routine during the fight, her favorite outfits, and how she engaged with the audience. That wouldn't be happening, not with the sheer outfit I had to wear. While she explained her extra duties in detail, I thought about Tyffani's alterations of illusion mesh and picked at a hangnail. She couldn't add enough fabric to make me comfortable. *It's fine. You only need to wear it for a couple of hours.* Several calming breaths helped.

Shelah showed me where to stand during the fights and the quickest routes to the offices. The harvester felt like a boulder, hidden under the arch of my foot. Even as I pretended to stretch out a cramp near Vujic's office, Shelah stayed with me, chattering non-stop. After several attempts, I gave up. I couldn't get close enough to download information.

Blaiz was waiting for me when I got home. It had become our new routine. At first, I thought he was lonely, then wondered if he was there because he'd just finished Grandma's deliveries. Earlier this week, she dismissed that theory. "He comes to visit even when I don't have any deliveries going out," she had said with a wink.

Butterflies swirled through my stomach at the memory. Something that looked very different from friendship was developing between us. The smile he gave me when I came home, the protective side he couldn't hide, the sparks that lit me up when our fingers brushed... I couldn't deny the attraction I felt. After this mess with Vujic was done, maybe we could spend some time together that wasn't overshadowed by scheming, fear, and anxiety.

Even as my heart lifted at the sight of his smile, I frowned. I'd failed to get what we needed.

"I'm sorry," I said as a way of greeting. "Although I walked by Vujic's office, I couldn't linger. How long did you say it would take?"

Blaiz put aside the book he was reading and met me in the kitchen. "A full minute, at the most. Relax. I know you did your best."

"I'll have to get the files tomorrow before the fight."

He poured me a glass of milk. "Don't rush. That's when mistakes happen."

"But this Saturday night, there's a big predator fight. Shelah said the crowd will be huge. Maybe with Vujic focusing on logistics, I'll be able to get the information."

Blaiz grabbed two napkins and put them on the counter. "We can move our plan to another weekend if we need to."

My life had become dominated by waiting—for the next encounter with my boss, the next disturbing request, the right moment to scrape incriminating data. After my first errand for Vujic, a lead ball had settled in my stomach, growing heavier with each passing day. "I don't know the fight schedule. It could be several weekends before another match."

"We can wait. While it'd be great to catch him in the act, you can't jeopardize your safety. Promise me you won't do anything risky," he said, his amber-eyed gaze pinning mine. The copper ring around his iris glimmered, his eyes turning gold. My heartbeat raced, and my face warmed. Despite my speeding heart, the concern in his expression had birds swooping in my stomach.

Clearing my throat, I pulled away before I did something stupid like kiss him. "Of course, I'll be careful, but maybe there's an easier way to get the information we need. Maybe I could go to his office—" I couldn't finish the sentence. Just the idea made me feel like throwing up.

"No." Blaiz's voice was a hard growl. His eyes flashed again before he cleared his throat. "The less direct contact you have with him, the better."

"If I asked him a question in his office, and he answered it, then that would probably be all the time I'd need to download the information." Even I could see how easy it would be. Unpleasant but efficient.

"Leave him alone, Ava. There will be other chances."

No, it had to happen within the next twenty-four hours. "How soon can peacekeeping forces move in after they receive the information?"

"Probably an hour or two. Ava, are you listening to anything I'm saying?"

"Of course I am," I said. Listening wasn't the same as agreeing. I changed the subject, my mind already made up.

The next night, I shoved down a piece of honey toast for supper, but everything tasted like ash. I arrived at Lodestar around six o'clock. A few people hung around the entrance, hoping to be the first in line. I slipped in through the back door in basic street wear. Tyffani had commed me earlier, saying she'd sent the costume to the arena by courier.

With every step, the harvester pressed into my foot. I ignored it and left it in my boot, hoping for the perfect opportunity. If it didn't happen soon, I'd have to get to Vujic's office right before the fight and make up a question to ask him.

An olive-skinned muscular man with exotic brown eyes and ebony hair waited near my dressing room, and I slowed my steps. What looked like armored plates decorated his black body suit. "Can I help you?"

"You're the new cage girl, right?" he asked.

Did Bran already place an officer on the inside? Without thinking, I said, "Yes, I am. Bran didn't mention you'd be here."

He squinted. "Bran? I don't think I've met him."

I fought against a catastrophic sinking feeling. Stupid, stupid, stupid. Whoever this guy was, he wasn't from peace-keeping. "You—you haven't?"

"Is he a new hire? I thought I met all the trainers on Thursday."

Before I could complicate things, he continued. "Not that I'll need them, of course." He gave me a flirty wink and held out a beefy hand. "I'm the house fighter tonight, Jaxon Oh."

I shook his outstretched hand, mentally berating myself. With another mistake like that, I'd ruin the entire plan.

I tuned in to hear his last sentence. "After I win tonight, maybe we could get a drink."

This guy had more confidence than Mo had fur. I pulled my hand free. "Thanks, but I already have plans. Besides, I'm not supposed to fraternize with the fighters." I wasn't sure if Shelah had said that, but it sounded like a good rule to follow.

He took my rejection with an amiable smile. "Let me know if you change your mind. Tell your *plans* he's a lucky guy."

I made my way into the dressing room. Did Blaiz consider himself lucky? I rolled my eyes. We weren't a couple. Aside from some meaningful eye contact, he hadn't held me in his arms or tried to kiss me. Maybe he wasn't interested, although the concern that sometimes slipped through his cynical mask made me wonder.

A box embossed with the WVE logo waited on a table next to the application center with an attached note. It was from Tyffani. *I think this uniform will meet with your approval. The boss might not be thrilled, but you won't get in trouble (and neither will I—I'm too good at my job!) Good luck at the fight tonight.*

I struggled into the costume, the Solknit dragging against my clammy skin. As promised, Tyffani had added a mesh panel to the neckline and a peplum-slash-train to cover the clinging pants that showed every wrinkle. After a quick appraisal, I began to tug it off. Wearing it during a meeting with Vujic was a bad idea. Even a quilted parka wasn't enough of a barrier between us. I'd wait until the last possible moment to get dressed for the fight in case I had a chance beforehand to get close to Vujic's office.

A comm came through, vibrating lightly under my skin. Vujic's name blinked on the small screen. *Come to my office. Wear the costume.*

Nausea rippled through my stomach. This was the perfect opportunity. Even though it was just an appearance inspection, I'd stay long enough to scrape his records. Unseen, the harvester lay in the arch of my foot in my boots. Nothing would keep it in place if I wore the sky-high heels that completed the outfit.

Biting my lip, I considered other hiding places as I slipped off my boots. There was no time to sew it into a cuff or slide it into an elaborate hairdo. As a last resort, I tucked it into the modified bra sewn into my outfit. A mirror check proved it wasn't noticeable. Slipping on the heels, I tottered off down the hallway toward Vujic's office, giving myself a pep talk the entire way. *I can be the unknown spy to ruin this monster. I'm the pretty face he'll never suspect. He'll never know what we've done until it's all over.*

I almost believed it until I knocked on the door of his office.

"Enter," he barked.

All my self-encouragement faded into a white blizzard of empty words.

As I stepped into the office, I avoided direct eye contact. He sat at his desk in an immaculately tailored black suit. My nose wrinkled at the spicy cologne wafting from him. The desk's inlaid screen showed the mostly empty arena in real-time. Workers moved among the aisles, preparing for the crowd that would arrive in a little over ninety minutes. Already a few VIP ticket holders trickled into the expensive box seats.

"You look absolutely stunning." He licked his lips as he stood from his seat. "I can see my choice was an excellent one. You'll make it difficult for my audience to focus on the fight, Ava."

My stomach flipped. "I prefer Avarill, Mr. Vujic. I mean, you're my employer."

Eyeing me like a piece of meat, he approached, his steps steady. "Surely you don't still feel like an employee here?"

I felt like a prisoner. "I haven't worked here that long."

My heart pounded as my eyes met his. The urge to cower, hide, escape grew. I froze under his hard blue gaze, my thoughts thrashing.

He trailed a hand down my arm. "This company is like a family."

Maybe a dysfunctional one. I jerked away, reminding myself why I was here. A sudden inspiration had me moving toward the livestream on his desk.

"Wow. You can see everything from here, even the box seats. How many people can this arena hold?" *Look here and stop tracking me. I'm giving you a chance to boast, you piece of garbage.*

There was only silence, and I wondered if I'd said my thoughts out loud. I turned to catch him ogling my backside. I cleared my throat.

Smirking, he moved toward me. "I like to keep up-to-date on the fights as they're played out. Tonight, we'll probably be at our twenty-thousand-seat capacity. Our house fighter, Jaxon, is an audience favorite. I'm expecting a sizeable crowd tomorrow night, too, since he'll be fighting again."

"He won't need time to recover?"

His suit jacket twitched with the slight shrug. "We have a backup fighter if Jaxon sustains a serious injury."

Stepping closer, he ran a stubby index finger along the illusion mesh at my low neckline.

I repressed a shudder as my skin crawled. The harvester was only a few inches below his disgusting touch.

"I don't remember asking for design changes here. Or here." He yanked on the train of material flowing from my waist, his hand almost touching me. "What is this?"

Taking a step back, I pulled the fabric from his reach, analyzing it like it was a petri dish growing mold. "I don't know. A peplum, I think it's called? I'll have to contact Tyffani—she did an amazing job with this costume."

"I believe it covers too much of your...assets." His insinuation dropped into the quiet room and swelled like a suffocating blanket.

Vujic again invaded my personal space. His eyes glowed, the brilliant blue gaze snaring and pinning me. The tight clench of danger filled my throat and chest and sent my internal alarms blaring. There was nowhere to run or hide—I was going to die in this basement office. I shifted closer to the door, my feet like lead. Hopefully, the harvester had picked up enough information because I couldn't stand being in this room with this monster any longer. "I didn't realize how late it is. I have to finish my hair and makeup."

Before he could stop me, I fled the office, my heart pounding and my eyes stinging.

It took a good half hour for my hands to stop shaking. Thankfully, the makeup application center put on my makeup. Otherwise, I would've stabbed myself in the eye with a makeup brush.

After finishing hair, makeup, and costume adjustments, I hurried to Andrija's office to escort Jaxon to the cage. Vujic's employees scurried through the hallways, each intent on making this first fight night perfect. Crowd noise filtered down from the seats, a rumbling murmur that grew louder or softer depending on my location in the tunnels.

Andrija gave me a smile when he answered the door. "Ready for an exciting night? Jaxon's ready to win."

Rising from his seat, Jaxon stretched before shaking out his shoulders. He was bare-chested, his muscles on full display. The waistband of his red Solknit shorts was emblazoned with the word Lodestar. "You're looking at a new champion, Avarill."

His cocky statement pulled a grin from me, despite my nerves. "Good luck."

As the three of us headed for the main tunnel, the crowd noise and aggressive music grew into a thunder. Energy filled the air as thousands of spectators waited for the fighters. Shelah had informed me during rehearsal that drinking and gambling were common on the floor. From where we waited, I caught glimpses of sweaty faces lit with greed, excitement, and alcohol. My stomach flipped. We hadn't even started, and I was ready for the night to be over. Andrija headed for Jaxon's corner as the presenter's voice boomed over the speaker.

"Ladies and gentlemen, we have an amazing presentation for you tonight. In one corner, we have our combatant hailing from Trystell's Zone Six. At one hundred ninety-eight pounds, he's won fifty-six fights with fifty-two knockouts. He's Trystell's gold medal heavyweight champion. Let's welcome Zaiden 'Meteor' Manolo!"

A man with bright red hair stepped onto the platform and raised his arms, no sign of nerves on his smirking face.

A wave of cheers, heckling, and boos drifted to where we waited. Jaxon bounced on his feet and flexed his wrapped hands.

The announcer continued, his voice rising over the shouting of the audience. "Our house fighter was born and raised in Cristalpeaks. He's Amaris's heavyweight gold medal titleholder. At two hundred pounds, he's shattered records with sixty-one fights and fifty-nine knockouts. Let's give a Lodestar welcome to the outstanding house fighter, Jaxon 'Jackhammer' Oohhhh!"

The crowd roared in response. As instructed, I tucked my hand in the crook of his elbow and led him to the raised dais in the center. With twenty-thousand sets of eyes marking our progress, I tightened my hold on Jaxon's forearm. People yelled and whistled, the sound blooming like a mushroom cloud. I met the eyes of the bouncer assigned for my protection. He gave me a brisk nod, and I released my hold on Jaxon's forearm. Everything was fine, even if I'd never been so uncomfortable.

We reached the platform. Before I stepped away, Jaxon grabbed my shoulders and pressed his lips to mine. Catcalls and whistles erupted from the crowd. Before I could push him away, he released me with a cocky smirk.

"What the suns was that?" I snapped.

"For luck," he stated with a wink as he stepped away.

I tucked my anger away. We'd be talking about that stunt later. Like Jaxon, I just needed to survive the next twenty minutes.

Chapter Eleven

Blaiz

THE GUY NEXT TO me whistled and then stumbled as he tossed back his drink. "Give me 'nother," he hollered. In seconds, the server pressed a fresh drink into his hands.

He elbowed me. "I've got three hundred puli riding on The Jackhammer. You wager anything?"

I shook my head. The clamor in the arena threatened to deafen me, and speaking without yelling was impossible.

As a spectator on the man's other side got his attention, my gaze drifted to Ava. If she was nervous, it didn't show. Her appearance at the beginning had stolen my voice—a vision in glistening scarlet Solknit. My chest grew tight as she stood at the platform's corner—anger, admiration, worry—it'd take a year to untangle all the feelings crowding me.

The fighters were tied. This third and final round would determine the winner, although Jaxon seemed to have the upper hand.

I eyed the holographic display clock hanging overhead. Only five minutes left. This fight had lasted for days, months, years, of observing Ava assist, cheer for, and watch Jaxon. My spirit wolf urged me to protect her, to whisk her away from this mess, and the feeling had only intensified as the minutes ticked away.

But that kiss. I flexed my hands. She hadn't mentioned Jaxon, although that didn't mean anything. Maybe it was better this way. She deserved someone who would protect her, not sell her out. I should've known—I'd never had a chance to begin with. I rubbed at the dull ache lying in my chest.

Bran had commed me when the information had come in from the harvester. Everything was ready. A fake report several pages thick rested in the inside pocket of my black jacket. As planned, after the fight, I would deliver it to Vujic, then Bran and his team would show up. The information received from the harvester had been solar—tax evasion, money laundering, smuggling, as well as human trafficking littered Vujic's records.

With a sudden surge, Jaxon rushed his opponent and landed several vicious blows. The visiting fighter's face already looked like a piece of raw meat. Jaxon delivered a final brutal strike. His opponent toppled and didn't get back up.

As the crowd erupted, throwing cups and paper advertisements into the air like confetti, the announcer joined in. "The winner of Fight Night One is Jaxon Oh!"

Jaxon grinned through his mouth guard, held up a hand in victory, and pulled Ava close to his side. Her eyes widened as Jaxon's trainer shoved the trophy at her. With a few more moments for newsfeeds reporting and clips, all three of them walked off the stage and into the underbelly of the arena.

I slipped from my seat, my usual adrenaline at the situation absent. The image of Jaxon holding Ava played on a loop in my brain. A professional fighter was a step up from a codestitcher with dirty DNA. I shook away the thought. Romance wasn't in the cards for me. I was here to trap Vujic, so I had to stay focused and not flare out just because the woman I'd dared to dream about would never be mine.

After skirting a few celebrating and drunk spectators, I headed for the tunnel. A guard stopped me at the entrance. "Authorized personnel only, pal."

"I'm here to see Vujic."

"Sure, ya are. And I'm the mayor of Cristalpeaks."

I allowed my alpha energy to rise to the surface, putting extra arrogance into my words. "Tell him Wild is here to see him with the requested information."

The man pulled back, his expression shifting to a frown. "If you say so."

He flipped open the protective shield on his BioDock and sent a comm. After a few moments, his eyes widened. "He says to head on back. Through here, turn right, continue on through the tunnels until they split and take the left fork. His office is on the left."

I jerked my head in thanks and left, my persona held in place with iron control. This way of carrying myself reminded me of my father and the way he would strut around our house like a king. Of course, this guise was my only defense if I was going to enter a dangerous world where Vujic was the biggest monster.

The tunnels deposited me at the shark's door, but voices from inside paralyzed me—Vujic's and Ava's. Why was she here? She should've been in her dressing room, or better yet, on her way home. I scanned the hallway for a good hiding place, somewhere to stay out of sight until Ava left.

Vujic's voice could cut glass. "Are you and Jaxon romantically involved?"

"No, we're not."

The relief that curled through me was short-lived.

"The crowd loved it. Let's play up that angle for tomorrow night. We'll leak some sexy engineered flixers of the two of you."

"But—"

Vujic's next words caught my attention. "One more thing before you finish for the evening. I want you to head out to Wolf's Maw."

"Wolf's Maw? Why?" Ava asked.

"Another operation. I've sent you the coordinates. I'm waiting for a colleague, but I'll meet you there. Don't be late."

Approaching footsteps sounded, and I turned back the way I came, weaving through the people crowding the hallways. If Ava saw me now, it would all be over. Time to pivot. I'd wait until she left and then give Vujic the information.

A drunken couple staggered for the main tunnel while a group of young men made plans to continue celebrating at a local club. Employees gave me curious glances until I allowed my shadow wolf to rise to the surface. When faced with the aura of a dangerous predator, they looked away and hurried down the tunnels. I found a small empty hallway to wait. Leaning into a shadowed corner, I pulled up an area map on my BioDock. A mining company had claimed acres and acres of forestland beyond Cristalpeaks. It shut down years ago, and the only thing around Wolf's Maw now was snow, trees, and a frozen pond or two.

A flash of red caught my eye. Ava hurried past. With a satisfied growl, I saved the coordinates and the map. Vujic wouldn't wait long. Before I could exit the hallway, he strode past my hiding place. My shoulders slumped. For an arrest to be made, Vujic needed to be holding the information, and I couldn't let Ava go to Wolf's Maw alone.

I escaped from the hallway and didn't take a full breath until I reached my vehicle. What was Vujic hiding at Wolf's Maw? Probably more criminal activity.

No way was I walking into Wolf's Maw without backup. I climbed into the wanderer and commed Bran to give him the details.

A blast of warm air from the wanderer's heating system filled the cockpit as Bran responded. "This wasn't the plan, Blaiz. My guys are already in place at Lodestar."

"Vujic instructed Ava to meet him at Wolf's Maw. I didn't have the chance to give him the false dossier." *Because I was a coward and didn't want Ava to see me.*

"We can't arrest him without the dossier."

"Yeah, I know. Sorry. They left as soon as the fight was over. He's already in the air. This is probably another of Vujic's underhanded deals you haven't uncovered. Get everything you can on him before he buries or hides it. You know half of these charges won't stick."

There was a moment of pregnant silence and then, "You're following them out there, aren't you?"

A whiteout couldn't keep me away, but I didn't tell Bran that. "I'll give him the dossier there. Location shouldn't matter much."

Bran sighed. "Right. Except for manpower and cover and the layout of the site. Fine. I'll send out instructions. Get there as fast as you can."

"I'm on my way there now."

"Right. Kethiran keep you," Bran said.

"You, too." I signed off. Something told me that even with the best circumstances, we'd need all the divine help we could get.

Wolf's Maw lay dark and silent, the old growth forest hiding secrets in the dappled moonlight. I'd parked the wanderer in an undisturbed clearing a half mile away. As I hiked my way in, I inhaled the crisp, pine-scented air. Noting I was downwind, I pulled harder on my enhanced sense of smell—at least four different males, maybe more. Definitely no Ava. Her unique sweet scent was never far from my memory.

At the abandoned mine, I tucked myself into a large copse of evergreens off to the side. Security lights lit the mine opening, and several men loitered outside. Vujic had found the perfect lair—there were no residents around for miles to see his new base of operations.

A massive crate with warnings stamped on the engrafted star steel panels stood front and center in an area of packed snow. Thick chains and stakes bracketed the crates. In the dark shadows of a lavender pine, I turned off my BioDock's audible setting and checked for new messages. Nothing. If Bran hadn't been able to work with the new plan, he would've commed me. The only thing left to do was watch and wait.

I pushed aside my worry as two of Vujic's associates approached the crate. The floodlights snapped on, and flapping and hissing came from inside. An armed, heavyset guy followed a bald man holding one of the biggest crowbars I'd ever seen.

"Open it up," the heavyset man said.

"Do you have the tranq dart?"

His colleague smirked. "You better hope so."

Another irritated hiss came from the container. A third man wearing stained overalls and rubber gloves grabbed the chained hook hanging from the crate's side. He clambered up on the top of the box. "Just open it enough so I can hook 'em."

After several tries, the crate side tilted open. The man dropped the hook through and then gave the thumbs up. "He's hooked. Go ahead and spring him."

When the crate opened, a stocky equine body laced with the head of an owl stepped from his cage with a flailing of wings. Each wing ended with a wicked pointed quill. Due to some unidentified DNA, above its large yellow eyes was an impressive set of sharp corkscrew horns.

When the animal reached the end of the chain, the restraints yanked him back. He brayed and kicked at the men in front of him, the muscular legs slashing the air.

The man on top of the crate scrambled down from his perch. "He's secure."

"Vujic wanted him inside," the heavyset guy said.

The man pulled off the rubber gloves. "He's a laced donkey. Do you want to wrangle him into that elevator?"

As if the mere mention conjured him, Vujic's large metallic wanderer arrived, followed by Ava's vehicle. After they parked, she stepped from her vehicle, dressed in her red cloak and warm thermic leggings. I kept hidden in my shadowed location, despite the pull to rescue her from this.

The moment she saw the creature, she swayed, bracing herself against a nearby tree for a moment.

She hurried to catch up as Vujic strolled toward the still-braying creature. "What is that?" Her soft voice carried to my hiding spot.

"That's our newest house fighter."

"He's laced. How are you going to get him to fight?"

"That's your job, Ava. I'm sure you have the necessary skills."

"I—I'm not sure what you mean. "

His smile was smug. "You thought I didn't know about your gift with animals?"

"But there's no way I can handle him. Getting near him would be suicide."

"Avarill." A threatening edge crept into Vujic's voice. "With your ability, you can and will do whatever I ask you to do."

Her shoulders slumped as she rubbed her temples.

"Why is the creature outside?" Vujic asked the workers.

They all eyed each other until the one holding the crowbar spoke up. "He's too big."

Vujic waved away the excuse. "He's under three hundred pounds. The shaft can handle him. Get him and the other creature inside."

"Do you want the other one out of the crate?" the heavyset man asked.

"Unbox him once he's transferred."

More workers emerged, all scurrying to carry out the boss's orders. Swaying where she stood, Ava's shoulders curled in as the animal fought the men.

Stiffening, Vujic turned toward my hiding place, his nose raised as if scenting the air. My stomach flipped. Unaugmented humans didn't have the developed sense of smell like wolves, so what was he doing? I froze as he studied the forest, his blue gaze like a laser.

"Inside," Vujic said, barely glancing at her. He hesitated and turned toward me.

My fingers inched toward my inner jacket pocket where I'd tucked a slimline directed energy weapon. While my mind flipped through fight-or-flight scenarios, the DEW waited as a last option.

After another tense minute, the man turned and disappeared into the mine. I commed a silent message to Bran.

Mark is already inside.

We're en route.

I gritted my teeth. I wanted an estimated time of arrival down to the second. Despite the less than helpful response, I turned off my BioDock and left my shadowy hiding space. I couldn't leave Ava down there alone with Vujic and whatever dangerous creatures he now owned. My inner wolf growled a warning—things were going to get bad fast.

As I sidled toward the entrance, the bite of cold steel pressed against the back of my neck. "One more move, and I'll ditch your dead body in the snow."

I clenched my jaw. There was no way to access the hidden DEW.

"Guess the boss really could smell a rat hiding in the trees," the man sneered as he slipped to my side. The bright entrance lights highlighted his wispy facial hair.

"I've got information Vujic has paid for."

He nudged the gun into my abdomen. "I could kill you and give him the information myself."

What an ice cadet. His actions and attitude proved he was unaware of the phaser I carried. He should've been wearing a weapons scanner. "Pal, if you kill me, I'm taking you with me."

"Yeah? You and whose army?"

I knocked the weapon out of his hand and grabbed his neck in an iron hold. His face blanched.

"Just me. Take me to Vujic, or I'll tear your throat out," I said, my voice low with the threat. As I released him, the guy scrabbled for his gun.

With a swift kick, I buried it in the snow. His gaze snagged on the way my hand drifted to my inner pocket. "Take me to your boss. Now."

Blinking, he licked his lips and hurried to the mine entrance. Despite the lengthy distance between us, he kept me in sight.

Inside the mine entrance was a lobby-sized area with a wide silver elevator. A line of blue lights lit the doorways, while warm gold floating squares near the ceiling illuminated the surrounding area. I followed him into the elevator and leaned against the far wall to watch him. He kept looking at me, then away as we smoothly descended. I grinned, allowing my wolf forward. With an audible swallow, the guy pressed his back against the elevator door. When we reached the bottom floor, the door slid open, and he rushed out.

The abandoned mine had been modified with higher ceilings. Forgotten scaffolding, plastic sheeting, and star steel rods littered a corner. The opened crates waited for transport on rails threading through the cavern. While Ava, Vujic, and several workers waited a short distance away from the elevator, the two laced creatures were chained against the far wall.

"Boss, this guy says he's got information for you."

As soon as I stepped out, my companion returned to the elevator, and it whisked him upwards.

Vujic turned, a question in his cold eyes. "Who are you?"

"I have the information you requested and paid for."

"You're late," he said, anger darkening his face. "I don't recall asking you to meet here. I waited for you in my office."

Ava had initially brightened at my arrival, her smile a ray of light struggling in the dark. I forced myself not to look at her. "You were busy when I arrived, with too many people in the hallways. Information only gets delivered in secure locations. This area is more secure."

A confused frown grew on Ava's face, and I pushed aside the growing ache in my chest.

His eyes flashed, and he held out a hand. "I'm the boss, Wild. Remember that. Hand over the information."

My spirit wolf snarled. Up close, I recognized that flash. Somehow, this lowlife had an augmentation like mine. My stomach rolled. With wolves, there could only be one alpha.

I pulled out the fake report stashed in an envelope. Vujic snatched it and leered at Ava. "This will tell me every detail I want to know about what you can do. So don't bother lying."

Her expression morphed from confusion to disbelief. "Wild?" Her voice broke.

It was a fine-bladed knife in my heart. This was where our relationship had always been headed, to this time when she would look at me like the garbage I was. If she used my name in front of Vujic, he'd figure out we knew each other.

I offered her a carefree smirk. "In the flesh. I take it you've heard of me."

Vujic finished skimming the report and looked up with a satisfied smile. "Excellent report, Wild. Your initial report proved invaluable in my acquisition of my new employee, who has an abundance of positive assets, don't you think?"

A hot flush rushed through my body. He had no right to look at her like that, but I had to play my part until Bran showed up. I pretended to check her out like the newest wanderer, but her beautiful attributes shone through—her kindness, her determination, her loyalty, her bravery. "*Very* nice," I said, the words thick on my tongue.

Her eyes... Hoarfrost. Her eyes glittered with hurt tears. Betrayal was etched on every beautiful angle of her face. She truly hated me. And I deserved it.

Chapter Twelve

AVARILL

I CLUTCHED MY ACHING stomach. Blaiz was Wild, the hacker who had handed me and my secrets to Vujic on a digital platter.

Why hadn't I made the connection? I'd been so gullible, assuming this gorgeous guy wanted to help me. He'd turned my attack at his doorstep into the perfect opening to create a connection. And I'd made it so easy for him, spilling every detail about how I'd received my ability and what it was like. Tears stung, a lump rising in my throat.

Nausea roiled as I remembered all the private thoughts and feelings I'd shared with him. I'd thought he was a friend, if not more. So, so stupid.

After that blistering look a few seconds ago that had stripped me naked, he hadn't turned my way again. I couldn't trust anything he'd told me—his computer business, the harvester, his brother on the peacekeeping force. I was alone, so I had to figure out my own escape.

"Would you like to see a demonstration of her ability?" Vujic asked Blaiz.

My head snapped up, and I looked at the creatures secured on opposite sides of the space. Although the chains held them in place, occasionally they'd pull and yank, and the restraints would tighten, like a finger trap. Aside from the donkey owl, there was also an alligator roach. The size of a paszec, it was an alligator head laced with the hard-shelled body of a cockroach. My stomach shuddered, and I looked away.

Blaiz leaned back against a support rod that disappeared into the striped rock walls. His shadowool jacket and black pants made him look every inch the villain.

I hate you. Leave me alone. Go away.

My subliminal message didn't work.

Blaiz shrugged, his gaze focused on the creatures.

Vujic took the movement as approval. "Avarill, show Wild how you control these animals."

I cleared my throat and refused to look at Blaiz. "That will be difficult when they're agitated."

Blaiz waved away Vujic's irritated frown. "A demo isn't necessary, but I'd like a closer look at those creatures."

Vujic shot me a glare before leading Blaiz toward the animals. I winced, a stab of pain spearing through my temples. With both creatures desperate and scared, their pain, anger, and terror filled my chest. A wave of dizziness assaulted me, and I leaned against the wall. As my emotions whirled, I struggled to remember something, anything, that would give me an edge in dealing with a laced creature.

Too soon, both of them returned. A strange expression filled Blaiz's face before he replaced it with a smug grin.

Vujic turned to me. "Now I want to see you control them."

Perhaps a delay would work. "I can't do anything until they've been fed."

"You'll do it now, or I'll find a position for you at the Nymph-house."

My stomach flipped, cold icing my limbs. I approached the alligator cockroach, studying it. When it began hissing, I slowed.

What was that piece of information about alligators? Something about getting them on their back?

"Stop stalling," Vujic said. "This most recent material unearthed by Wild confirms my suspicions. Communicate with them."

It was another icepick in my heart. *Communicating* was a bit of a stretch, but of course, Wild wasn't an honest guy. As I buried my hurt, I remembered the interesting fact. Hopefully, this laced creature was more alligator than roach.

Spying a two-foot rod of star steel at my feet, I grabbed it. It would do as a weapon. When I approached the alligator roach, it lunged and snapped. I blocked it with the rod, then slipped the end under his belly and pulled up. The creature flipped. Rushing to its side, I put all my weight on its head, pressing it into the floor to prevent its jaw from opening. Surprise and confusion, then panic, filtered through to me. The seconds seemed to slow. Although Vujic was yelling something behind me, I ignored him until the animal went limp.

I stood, stumbling as the animal's emotions faded.

"What was that?" Vujic's face had turned an ominous shade of red. "Did you kill it?"

"No. Tonic immobility. It means he fainted. He'll be fine."

Vujic snorted. "That's animal handling. I want to see communication. Talk to them, Avarill. Release the other creature and command it to bow at my feet."

I couldn't talk to animals, and Blaiz knew it. Why would he make up a lie like that? I winced as the donkey owl wildly flapped its wings. Desperate thoughts of swift flights and safe forests filled me. My eyes stung, and I blinked to keep the tears from falling. "I don't know if I can."

Vujic stalked toward me, grabbed my jaw, and dug his fingers in. "You will. I've spent money, turning you into my asset. I don't lose money, Avarill."

My stomach cramped at his words. He didn't look away, his gaze pinning me in place. Tremors took hold, and my heart rate increased. As a growl rumbled from his chest, his eyes promised a slow, painful punishment.

Run. Now.

"Okay." Jerking away, I stumbled toward the donkey owl. Several deep breaths helped, but the creature froze, his beak clicking as he picked up on my emotions.

"A-aren't you a pretty girl?" I closed my eyes as another wave of fear swamped me. This was a disaster. I tried again, using my most calming voice. "You and I are going to become friends, so you need a name." A sudden idea caused hope to ignite in my heart. "You look like a Karis to me." The name of my best friend, someone I loved, would help control my rising fear.

Behind me, Vujic laughed. "Naming the animals already, Avarill? These aren't pets. They're my fighting machines."

A few workers laughed too, but I ignored them all.

Was this creature more donkey or owl? Hopefully, there wasn't much wild goat in the DNA mix, although its horns were impressive. I mentally burrowed past the fear flooding the animal and sent images of dark forests, kind voices, and warm, gentle touches on its shoulder. "I won't hurt you, Karis. We can help each other."

The donkey owl didn't move, and I reached out, placing a hand on its lower neck where the feathers mingled with its stubby mane. At contact, the skin rippled, but she didn't lash out. "That's it. Such a good girl."

Vujic, Wild, and the other workers were quiet as I located the simple latch for the chain. After releasing the chain, I slowly led the creature from where she'd been restrained. "That's it." Several strokes calmed her more, although the creature's wide, yellow eyes were spooky up close.

A low rumble from above shuddered through the cavern, but I continued to pet the animal's shoulder. Her neck dropped, relaxing.

When we were about ten feet away from Vujic, I sent another image, this one of my boss in the most threatening pose I could imagine. *Danger.*

The donkey lowered its horns at Vujic but didn't bolt. As I led her closer, I imagined Vujic's face changing into that of a wolf.

Danger, I told the creature again. Terror and fear pulsed through the connection I had with the laced animal. I bit back a curse. It could just as easily run away instead of attacking. Before I could try anything else, the donkey owl charged and then kicked.

One of the animal's hooves struck Vujic's chest, sending him sliding into the wall. The man slumped to the floor and clutched his chest, his face dazed and pale.

The elevator opened, disgorging a dozen armed men. "Peace-keeping," a muscular guy with brown hair shouted. "Drop your weapons!"

The next moments fused into a chaotic whirl of movements and sound. From his place on the floor, Vujic reached inside his suit jacket. Blaiz shoved me behind scaffolding draped in plastic and covered me with his body as the cavern erupted in a barrage of phasers firing.

Blaiz lowered his head to mine. "It's okay, Ava. I've got you."

He grasped my hands and tucked me close. I couldn't help curling into a ball, his chest a safe shelter. Why would he protect me? And why was I letting him?

Several shots ricocheted over our heads, chipping off shards of rock. One fragment bit into my neck, and I hissed in pain. Blaiz jerked, and he gripped my hand tighter. Waves of intense panic sent my heart racing. I broke out in a cold sweat.

"It's almost over," he whispered.

I clenched my jaw, my mind creating detailed escape plans and ignoring the fact we might die here. But we couldn't—I had to keep *her* safe. What?

A headache bloomed above my right eye. With a frown, I chanced a look at Blaiz, and his eyes flashed gold before he lowered his face into the curve of my neck. Mint and a whiff of incoming snow surrounded me. I curled in closer to his scent, knowing I'd hate myself for this moment later. With a sudden shout, the noise stopped.

An officer yelled, "Got him."

The peacekeeping personnel moved in to arrest the criminals and check for injuries.

"Blaiz, let go." I wiggled out from under his dead weight. As I pushed him away, my hands slipped, coated in red sticky liquid.

I gasped. Looking for the wound, I palmed my chest and waist. Although I couldn't find an injury, my head and shoulder ached, and blood soaked my shirt sleeve.

Groaning, Blaiz struggled to sit up. I glanced over, zeroing in on the red stain spreading from his shoulder and down his chest.

My head spun. There was so much blood. I scooted closer and slipped an arm around his shoulder. "Blaiz, you're hurt."

An officer reached us, his eyes concerned. "Man down. We need a physipad," he called to another officer.

Blaiz met my gaze, his eyes still glowing with gold sparks.

My heart thundered in response. "It's okay," I forced the words out. "They'll get you fixed up."

When his fingers brushed my neck, I flinched at the sting. His face blanched. "You're bleeding."

I touched the area, and my hand came away smeared with blood. A brief flash of shame rocketed through me, and my headache took on a pounding edge. "It's not bad. You—you protected me. Why?"

A random surge of relief left me lightheaded as Blaiz briefly closed his eyes. My emotions were all over the place—maybe the laced animals were in shock and affecting me. I leaned in. "Blaiz?"

An officer with a first aid pack withdrew a physipad and used it on Blaiz before pulling out a sheet of Restorscreen. "This should hold until we can get you looked at." As he applied it to the wound, Blaiz hissed, his face rigid.

Pain shot through my shoulder before disappearing like a phantom.

Blaiz grabbed my hand, then slumped against the wall. His eyes slid closed.

"It's okay, ma'am," said an officer as he used the physipad to treat my aches and pains. As the warming sensation flowed over me, my headache eased. The man applied a small gauze bandage to my neck. "He's passed out. We'll get him a doc at Cristalpeaks' Medical Services Center."

"There's so much blood," I said numbly.

He gave me an understanding nod. "A little blood makes it look worse than it is."

Two officers loaded Blaiz onto a drift panel. As they guided it into the elevator, I stood up and scanned the cavern.

Vujic's colleague, Kacic, was dead. After the emergency medical personnel wrapped Vujic's chest, the cops handcuffed him to another drift panel. As an officer led the criminals from the cave under heavy guard, several other officers prepared the laced animals for transport.

I glanced down at the blood drying on my sleeve. Blaiz had protected me when the shooting started. Was it because he felt guilty for his betrayal, for putting both me and my grandmother at risk? Did Bran know Blaiz had sold my information to Vujic? Had there really been a plan to trap Vujic, or had his brother shown up by coincidence? Was anything about Blaiz true? I felt used, not just by Vujic, but by the man with a ruthless heart of a wolf.

The muscular officer assigned a team to move the animals. He made his way over to where I leaned against the rough rock wall.

The man ran a hand through his chestnut hair, his broad shoulders set in weary lines. "Hi, you must be Avarill. I'm Bran, Blaiz's brother."

I raised my eyebrows. At least that much had been true. "Blaiz speaks of you often."

Bran gave me a tired grin, his smile so much like his brother's, it hurt a little to see it. "We have to take you in since you're a witness. We can release you after you give a quick testimony."

The hours before I could go home stretched before me. "I'd like to comm my grandmother so she doesn't worry."

"We can do that for you." Bran asked a colleague to send a comm, then directed him to take me to the station.

At the station, I waited for an officer in a nondescript gray room. The break gave me time to brood about my fluctuating responses in the mine. I'd felt extreme determination and panic, followed by shame and relief. And there had been the need to save an unnamed *her* and the phantom pain in my shoulder. Only one explanation made sense. The wild reactions I felt in the mine had been Blaiz's. His wolf DNA allowed me to connect with that part of him. The intimacy of that interaction was just another layer added to my conflicting feelings about Blaiz.

Despite Bran's promise, it was early morning by the time they released me. One of the peacekeeping members had flown my wanderer to the station so I could fly home. I was approaching twenty-four hours without sleep. I was grimy, my eyes gritty, my makeup gone. A cup of barzina and half of a sketchy ham and cheese sandwich barely kept the hunger at bay. Once I got home, I planned to collapse and sleep for a long, long time.

Trudging down the vivid white hallway of the station, I spun my fantasy of sleeping for hours. I imagined multiple pillows, soft sheets, and cozy flannel blankets.

Bran caught me as I reached the exit. "I wanted to thank you for your part in this. If it hadn't been for your willingness to wear the harvester, Vujic would still be a free man."

"So that was real, huh?"

He frowned. "Of course, it was real. Blaiz said he explained the plan, and you agreed. He told you, right?"

"I'm a bit confused about what's real and what's a lie. Your brother's talented at sharing half-truths." I closed my eyes briefly. Bran wasn't the enemy, and I was cranky. "I'm glad you got the information you needed. Will it keep Vujic in jail?"

"After capturing the laced animals and seeing the financials for the fighting ring, even a talented lawyer won't be able to get him out of this. He'll be going away for a good, long time."

"Glad he's finally paying for it," I said.

I turned to go, but his voice stopped me. "Avarill?"

He opened his mouth, closed it, then tried again. "You and Blaiz had a rough night. Things will look different tomorrow. He's a good guy. Give him a chance."

His words triggered the raw hurt I'd been ignoring. "To what? Betray me again? He sold my private information to a disgusting worm. I was sexually harassed and then black-mailed into taking a job so we wouldn't lose our home. All because Vujic knew my secrets, thanks to your brother."

Bran frowned. "Vujic was a holdover from his old list of clients. He's not dealing with criminals anymore and has turned his life around."

"Well then, let's give him a free pass," I said, my sarcasm thick. "Just because Vujic was finally caught doesn't erase the harm done to my family. The end doesn't justify the means."

Bran tucked his hands into his pockets. "Right. Well, get the full story from him before you decide to break his heart."

Turning, he walked back into his office and left me standing in the hall.

Break Blaiz's heart? My heart was already in pieces, left behind in an abandoned mine.

The flight home was a blur. I entered the cottage quietly, but Grandma Hannah roused from her chair, her eyes springing open. "Ava, you're home. You're hurt," she said, staring at my neck and my blood-soaked sleeve.

"It's just a scratch. Most of the blood is Blaiz's. He got shot, but he's okay." *I hoped*. "They took him to Medical Services."

"What happened?" She couldn't seem to stop staring at my bloody sleeve.

There was no way I was giving her an in-depth account of how we tricked Vujic. Maybe later, when the horror wasn't so fresh, I could share more with her. "Peacekeeping forces arrested Vujic last night after the fight. Blaiz's brother says he'll be put away for good."

Looking up, she pressed her hand to her heart. "Finally."

A wave of fatigue swept over me. I swayed and slouched against the wall, my eyes feeling like they were full of sand.

Grandma's sharp gaze missed nothing, and she moved to my side. "I'm thankful you're safe. Let's get you to bed. You need your sleep after such a dreadful night."

I didn't argue. In minutes, I'd stripped and fallen into bed. Mo's flowing, furry tail thumped against me as I fell asleep.

I slept for twelve hours straight. Grandma greeted me with a tight hug when I came downstairs, concern darkening her eyes.

She pulled away with a frown. "I stayed up as long as I could last night, even after that nice officer told me you were fine and to get some sleep. Can you tell me what exactly happened?"

After releasing a giant yawn, I told her about the evening, from the fight to the events at Wolf's Maw. "They arrested Vujic and his cronies. One of the peacekeeping officers said I'm out of a job, though."

"I can't believe you took such a risk. If I had known—"

"That's why I didn't tell you. I was one of the few people who could do it."

Grandma frowned. "Hmph. Well, what you did was dangerous, but thank Kethiran you're safe."

We entered the kitchen, and I poured myself an enormous glass of milk. "I don't know what will happen to the mortgage. I can go back to making deliveries next week. If I need to get a better-paying job, though, I will."

Her brow furrowed. "Do you enjoy making deliveries? I've never asked."

"I do," I assured her. "It's fun catching up with the regulars and meeting new people. The tips are always nice, even if I'm not making a lot of money." We wouldn't get rich, like a certain guy I knew. Hmm, extra cranky sarcasm. I needed more sleep.

I gathered the ingredients for an omelet—cheddar cheese, bacon, and tomatoes.

Grandma cracked eggs into a bowl. "Blaiz called a couple of hours ago. He wanted to talk to you."

I frowned as my traitorous heart leaped once before I hammered it into submission. "I don't want to talk to him." Not now and maybe not ever, although Bran's words echoed in my mind.

"That's your choice." Her tone of voice suggested maybe it wasn't the best one.

"Is he okay?"

She gave me a knowing look. "The shot just grazed him. He's fine and already recovering."

"Oh. Good." I shredded the cheese into a bowl.

"You could call him and discover this information yourself."

I forced a fake smile. "I don't need to. You already told me."

Grandma pursed her lips, but I ignored her look of disapproval. She didn't understand. She hadn't fallen in love with him.

I stilled, scowling at the pile of cheese. No. Just no, that's not what I'd done. I bit down a groan. Had I become so lonely and pathetic I'd fallen for a two-faced criminal? But the guy in the mine wasn't the same guy I'd had honey cakes with in our kitchen. Was Blaiz the sweet guy who'd helped my grandmother, or the crooked codestitcher who sold my secrets? Perhaps I'd never know the true Blaiz.

I finished cutting up the tomato and turned to Grandma. "Do you want some of the omelet?"

She held up a hand, palm out. "No, you eat it all. You're getting too skinny."

With an eye roll, I dropped a few pieces of bacon for Mo, and the paszec rewarded me with a wave of love and joy.

I spent the day playing card games with Grandma, reading, and doing laundry. The remarkably quiet day felt wonderful. My mind wasn't so silent.

What about Blaiz? Maybe I should contact him.

Absolutely not.

Wouldn't it be fair to hear his side of the story?

No, there was no excuse for his behavior.

What about the way he covered me when the shooting started? He was shot protecting me.

Big deal. He still sold you out.

Each hour, the argumentative voices had gotten louder, my conscience encouraging me to hear him out before I settled into righteous anger. But Vujic had known Blaiz and called him Wild, the same name of the person who'd sold my secrets. Blaiz hadn't denied stealing and selling my medical files. This wasn't a misunderstanding.

As I prepared for bed, I remembered the way Blaiz had thrown himself over me. He'd tucked his head next to mine and whispered in my ear, *It's all right, Ava. I've got you.*

My heart spasmed. He got me for sure. Was that part of the role? Or was that the real Blaiz?

Chapter Thirteen

AVARILL

A WEEK LATER WHEN the weather warmed, Mo and I hiked up the trail behind our house. The crisp day boasted a hard blue sky, and the sun shone so brightly the snow sparkled like diamonds.

Mo hopped through the drifts, chasing squirrels and other small animals. Their fear at being chased were quick flashes as Mo lost interest and kept returning to check on me. After one such check, the brush rustled behind me. Mo must've tracked a squirrel into the clearing. Turning, I found Blaiz.

A soft, cobalt scarf looped around his neck, tucked into the front of his lined shadowool jacket. He shoved his hands deep in his pockets. His long bangs were wind tousled.

His amber eyes locked on my face as we drank each other in. "Sorry. I didn't know you were here," he said and turned to leave.

"Wait." I searched for the courage and the right words.

He froze before turning back around, the small light of hope in his eyes almost painful.

"How do you feel?" I asked.

"I've recovered. It was just a graze that bled a lot."

"I'm glad you're okay," I said, surprised to find it was true.

Awkwardness seeped into the moment. "I haven't seen you since Friday night," I said.

A muscle twitched in his jaw. "Consider yourself lucky. Wasn't that what you wanted?"

"What I want is to understand. When I left the peacekeeping office, Bran said I should talk to you. Any idea why he would say that?"

His lips twisted. "He's trying to fix our friendship. I'm not expecting your forgiveness."

My heart sank at his use of the word friendship. "Why?"

"I can't forgive myself." Disgust coated each word. "As usual, I flared out. I'm sorry."

I sat down on the rock and pointed to the empty spot next to me. "Then help me understand. Why did you sell my information to Vujic?"

He sat, leaving acres of space between us. "There's no explanation that excuses what I did."

"Fine. I don't want excuses and half-truths. Tell me everything."

He sat forward with a sigh, his elbows on his knees. "I'm a codestitcher. I create code, alter programs, and uncover information people want to keep hidden. For a long time, I worked for guys just like Vujic, some who were associates of my father's. They wanted someone who could bury or access information for business or personal reasons, often blackmail. About six months ago, the peacekeeping force arrested one of my clients. Bran said my handle came up during his confession."

"Handle?" I asked.

"It's my username. Codestitchers never use their first or last names."

"So, Wild, then."

He glanced at me, before focusing on the snow at his feet. "Yeah. Bran came to talk to me and accused me of being no better than our dad. He was right. I was following in his footsteps. Bran's supervisor realized I'd be an asset to them, so he offered me a deal—go straight and freelance for the force or go to jail."

"That sounds like blackmail."

He shrugged. "No, it was a plea agreement. I was more than willing to walk away from that life. Every day, I became more like my father, someone I hated. Before I tossed my old client list and went straight, I finished Vujic's job and never looked back. He said you owed him money and wanted your secrets dug up. I did it and thought that was the end."

"Until I got attacked outside your house."

"When you told me your name, it shocked me. I'd never met my marks." He tucked his head and mumbled something into his coat collar.

I leaned forward. "What?"

"We never should've met."

Wow. And I didn't think I could hurt worse than I already did. "I see."

"No, you don't." He huffed out a breath. "I've done nothing but hurt you and your family. I sold your secrets, put both of you at the mercy of a criminal, let you take part in a sting to bring him down—"

"Excuse me, I chose to take part in getting Vujic arrested."

He frowned. "I wanted to keep you safe, far away from Vujic. And I failed."

"Blaiz, no one forced me. There wasn't anyone who could've done what I did, since I was an employee. I'm proud of it. Not that I want to do it again, of course."

The look Blaiz shot me indicated he thought I was sunspotted. I ignored it. "So, you sold my secrets to Vujic and then we met. Anything else?"

"My first thought was you didn't look like the criminals I usually dealt with, and well, I assumed you used your looks in your cons."

I raised an eyebrow. "Blaiz, that makes no sense. Blue-eyed blondes are pretty normal around here."

"None of them look like you. You're beautiful. But my shadow wolf has good instincts. He—he never reacted to my other clients like that."

Beautiful. Heat filled my cheeks at the casual way he brought it up, like it was common knowledge. And what was his shadow wolf? Another question I needed an answer to. "You could've just let me go and never contacted me again."

He frowned. "I couldn't. At first, I wanted to figure you out. How had you crossed Vujic? But after talking with you and after seeing the way Vujic looked at you, I knew you needed help. You were his target, not a fellow criminal."

"When was this?"

"When he came and offered you the job."

Hunching my shoulders, I shoved my hands deeper into my coat pockets. The helplessness and fear of that day would take a while to fade. "You heard that? Weren't you out in the glass house?"

He dropped his gaze. "I followed your grandmother in, but I hid in the kitchen like a coward."

Although I would've loved to have him standing next to me while I faced down Vujic, there wasn't much he could have done. Mo wandered over to me and settled on my feet. "It's probably for the best, otherwise our plan wouldn't have worked."

He conceded the point with a nod of his head. "It would've made it a lot harder. So anyway, I'm sorry—for everything. I know it changes nothing, but if I could go back and do it over, I'd return Vujic's money and shut my doors."

I scratched Mo behind his ears, and he leaned his furry body into my legs. "Why did you lie and tell Vujic I could communicate with animals?"

A muscle jumped in his jaw. "We needed something to pull Vujic in. He wanted as much information on you as I could get. He even asked for personal details on your grandma."

I gasped, but he shook his head. "We gave Vujic a false report and posted an officer at your house for protection."

"Oh. I never saw him."

His lips quirked. "That means he did a good job, although he wasn't there long."

"You mentioned your shadow wolf. Does that have to do with the wolf DNA you have?"

"Yeah. The DNA has created something like a spirit or a shadow inside that's focused mostly on instincts. While it gives me improved senses like smell and sight, he's not great in polite society. I can ignore him if I have to."

He stared at the town of Skift below. "Anyway, at the mine, I knew you'd figure out I was the dirty codestitcher who'd sold your information."

At the reminder, I waited for my anger to ignite, but after a quick spark, it faded. He'd been caught between his old life and his new choices. It was easy to feel self-righteous and angry, but what if I'd been in the same situation? Would I have made a similar choice?

"So, you were okay with me finding out?"

"Not really, but if it meant Vujic wouldn't be able to hurt you anymore, I could deal with you hating me."

My chest splintered. He'd given up on himself. As if he would always be nothing but a *dirty codestitcher*, no matter what he did. As if no one could ever see him differently. "If things had gone as planned, I would've never found out who you were."

"And we would've had a chance," he said, his voice quiet.

My stomach fluttered. While I wanted to follow up on that comment, I had to address the lying. "I can't trust you if you're not being honest, Blaiz. I don't trust this Wild guy. He's, uh, kind of a jerk."

Blaiz barked out a surprised laugh. "Yeah, I wish I could leave Wild behind me and just be Blaiz."

"So do that."

He turned to glare at me. "Apparently, I can't. My past will never stay buried. I can't just wish for more. I've made too many wrong choices."

The defeat in his voice pulled at my chest. "No, that's not true. You've already made positive changes. Just focus on the future."

"I can't do that with a past like mine."

"But isn't that where it is? In the past? You can leave it behind, Blaiz." I almost reached out to touch him, but instead, I clasped my hands together in my lap.

Even though he had hurt me, I understood. His actions hadn't been an attack on me but on a faceless person who he assumed was a criminal just like Vujic. Blaiz was moving forward, but he couldn't see past his mistakes. I wanted to be the one who held up the mirror so he could see the man he was becoming.

Swallowing hard, he studied me, as if the truth was painted on my face.

I considered my next words. Time for a little bravery. "I like Blaiz. He's a good guy. A little cynical, but still a good guy."

"I lied to you, betrayed your trust, put you and your grandmother in jeopardy."

"Your sales approach needs some work."

"Look, I'm damaged, not just because of my augmentation, but because of my past. You should walk away. Friends don't sell out friends." Pain rolled off his words, the way he tried to create space between us.

I studied him, trying to guess how he'd respond to my words. There wasn't a way to ease into it. "I think we're more than friends. I can connect with your wolf."

His expression went blank. "What?"

"At the mine, I could feel your emotions. I felt your determination to protect me, your anxiety during the fight, the shame when you saw I was bleeding. I felt it all."

Wincing, he pinched the bridge of his nose. "Hoarfrost, that's messed up. That's a perfect sign you should move forward with your life, make friends with someone normal."

"I'm not interested in someone normal. I'm interested in this guy with wolf DNA who's protective, helpful, and caring."

Blaiz continued to study the palms of his hands.

My heart plummeted. Well, that was embarrassing. I couldn't figure this guy out. He talked about the two of us having a chance, then he mentioned friendship. Which was it?

Either way, I knew what I needed to do. "I forgive you, Blaiz. As long as you promise to stop the lies and half-truths."

"Just like that, huh?"

I nodded once. "Just like that."

He looked at me for a long moment. "I can do that. I knew from the beginning I should tell you, but I didn't know how."

It wouldn't have gone well, but I kept that information to myself. "I don't mind hard conversations. I'm not rich, but honesty is a currency I don't skimp on."

With a frown, he nodded. "Well, speaking of rich, I am."

"Yeah, I remember your offer to buy Grandma and me a house. Are we talking about a tiny house or an enormous mansion?"

"A mansion. I made enough puli in my illegal codestitcher days to live the rest of my life without working. That's why I made the offer. Money isn't an obstacle. I could buy your neo-res outright, so your grandmother and you always had a home. Or

I could build you a new one. Or we could travel. We could visit Isvora or old friends of yours in Ramilion."

His eyes dropped to my lips before he cleared his throat. "I mean, if you wanted to. Obviously, you can do what you want—" He tucked his hands in the pockets of his jacket.

If I looked closely, it seemed his cheeks were a touch pinker than usual. I bit back a smile. The big, tough guy could blush.

I gave him a mock glare. "Are you friend-zoning me, Blaiz?"

"No! I mean, if that's what you want, or—" He groaned, closing his eyes for a long moment. His long eyelashes made smoky shadows on his cheeks.

With an audible exhale, he turned to me. "What do you want, Ava? If you want to be friends, I can do that."

"What if I want more?"

One of his hands covered mine, his touch causing warmth to pool in my chest. "Yeah?"

I nodded. "I probably owe you my life."

His eyes glittered, the heat in them erasing my brain activity. "How so?"

"Um." *What were we talking about?* "You—you shielded me when the shooting started. Even though I kind of hated you, I also felt safe. Maybe deep down I knew who the real Blaiz was."

He traced my jaw, a smile playing at the corners of his mouth. "I can work with a life debt. Let's say repayment is one kiss a day. Does that work for you?"

"Just one?"

"Are you always so greedy?" he asked with a grin.

I grasped the front of his jacket with both hands and tugged. "Do you always talk so much?"

His amber eyes flashed, then his mouth covered mine, warm in the chilly air. Goosebumps raced across my skin as one of his hands tunneled through the hair at my nape.

One kiss down and thousands more to go.

Epilogue

Blaiz

Ava and I arrived on Ramilion at twilight. The double suns, on their way toward the horizon, blasted like the inside of an antimatter-fired oven. To my left, the Trivashan Castle's twisting, double pinnacle glittered, and waves of white sand stretched beyond the city on my right.

Although the interplanetary portals were convenient, using them made my spirit wolf anxious. I relished the sensation of standing on solid ground and gave a parting glance to the gated, glowing circle. We pressed through the milling crowd waiting their turn to travel to one of the other planets.

A trickle of sweat slipped down my spine. A light, early evening breeze offered a brief respite.

Ava turned to smile at me, and I forgot the heat, where we were, my name. That happened a lot. I still couldn't believe how lucky I was to have her next to me. After the fiasco six months ago, it was a miracle she'd forgiven me.

"So, what's the plan?" I asked. After asking too many questions about her life on Ramilion, Ava finally arranged a trip for the two of us to visit the sister planet. Although I didn't say it, I would've followed her anywhere. I was happy just being by her side.

After linking hands, we sat on a nearby public bench. Ava turned to me. "My best friend Karis is meeting us here. You two will probably have a lot in common."

"How so?"

"How much do you know about the Kali?" she asked instead.

"Is this a topic change?

She shook her head. "This is related, really."

I shrugged. "Bran said they're responsible for the protective shield around the peacekeeping office. It's a nifty piece of Kali tech."

Ava nodded. "Right. Karis is Kali. All Kali have magical gifts. She's gifted at dealing with augmented computers, enhanced firewalls, encryption, the kinds of things you deal with every day."

"That's an interesting combination. Still, I'd rather ask her about all the childhood trouble you got into."

"There isn't any," she said with a fake haughty sniff. "I was an angel."

Smirking, I leaned toward her. "Yeah, my angel," I said, my lips brushing against the shell of her ear.

She gave a small shiver. I swallowed a smile. I'd have to explore that further the next time we were alone.

As I pulled away, someone called her name.

A pretty Kali female with the typical pastel shaded skin waved and jogged over, her brown hair bouncing with each step. "Ava! It's so good to see you! Suns and moons, it's been like two years, right?"

"At least," Ava said as she gave her friend a big hug.

The woman pulled away, her dark eyes studying me. "You must be Blaiz."

Without waiting for my response, she turned to Ava. "Girl, you've been holding out on me."

Blushing, Ava grinned. "I told you I was seeing someone."

"Hi," I said and shook her hand. Meeting strangers made me nervous, but my shadow wolf gave a tail wag, serene in Ava's presence. Shortly after we started dating, the animal began muttering about mates. At first, I'd ignored him. I wouldn't screw up one of the best things in my life just because of pressure from my headstrong wolf. But something had shifted in the last month.

Tell her now, he ordered.

Kinda in the middle of something here. It's called small talk.

With a low growl only I could hear, he withdrew to a far corner of my consciousness with his back to me. Fine. I didn't want to talk to him either.

Two elite members of the Trivashan peacekeeping force marched by, their white uniforms glowing in the twilight, and Karis's face shifted to a sickly green hue. She pulled up her headscarf, hiding most of her features. "We need to go. Follow me." She turned down a sidewalk away from the portal.

My wolf perked up at the rush of anxiety. "Is everything okay?"

Karis shook her head. "Later. Have you two eaten?"

"We did," Ava said. "You don't even need to fix breakfast for us tomorrow. We can grab something from a restaurant or kiosk."

Karis gave her a mock glare. "You will not. I'd love to make you a full breakfast. When was the last time I cooked for you?"

"It's been a long time." Ava directed her next comment to me. "She's an amazing cook. And when she and her brother cook together, magic happens."

Karis's face crumpled, but she turned away before Ava noticed.

It took only minutes to reach her wanderer, parked in a municipal parking lot. After storing our luggage, Karis set the coordinates for her home and relaxed as the wanderer lifted off.

Ava settled in next to me, her warmth welcome against my side. "How is Karden?" she asked.

Her friend's dark eyes welled with tears. "Sorry. I didn't want to tell you not to visit, but this last week has been rough."

"What do you mean?"

"My brother's missing." With several rapid blinks, Karis focused on the wanderer's instrument panel.

"Missing?"

Karis bit her lip. "Karden was overdue returning from a trip to Isvora, so we accessed his BioDock data. It showed a timestamp from the Ramilion portal that evening, but he never came home. Although our empir is doing what he can, Karden disappeared on Trivashan land. The Itsavden forces are limited to our region."

As Ava squeezed her hand, Karis wiped her eyes. "Karden isn't the only one. There have been at least half a dozen other Itsavden citizens who are missing, too. I keep praying the Moon Goddess will keep him safe."

Ava leaned forward. "Have you asked the Trivashan peace-keeping force for help?"

The color leached from Karis's face, making the pastel colors more noticeable. "They aren't friendly toward the Kali. Especially since their empir died."

I frowned. "I'm sorry. This was a bad time for a visit."

Karis offered a small smile. "No, don't be silly. With the worsening drought and my worry over Karden, your visit is a bright spot I needed."

With a mischievous grin, she eyed Ava. "And the fact you came with a friend? That's even better."

A blush tinted Ava's cheeks. I tucked her closer to my side. We were more than friends, and we both knew it. I'd passed that point in our relationship four months ago. She was The One for me.

Karis's residence was a beautiful two-story house with an enclosed central courtyard and garden. Red terra cotta and elaborate tile work filled her home, alcoves filled with vivid flowers in shades of burgundy, purple, and pink. Despite our assurance that we'd already eaten, she still put out a snack of cheese, crackers, and fruit. We sat next to the courtyard's reflecting pool filled with floating lanterns and talked as the stars came out overhead.

The evening passed quickly. Ava and Karis talked with the ease of old friends and pulled me into their childhood stories and inside jokes. The sour trace of fear following Karis eased, and Ava's eyes lit with laughter as they talked. By the time we parted ways for bed, I felt like I'd made a friend.

It was late when I lay down in a guest bedroom. Closing my eyes, I tried to relax. I gave up an hour later. I was still keyed up from the trip, and my brain kept spinning theories about Karden's disappearance. Karis's worry had been the unspoken guest tonight, the acidic scent obvious to my wolf's sense of smell. Unfortunately, the only things to be done were to wait and pray.

I pulled on the pair of pants I'd worn earlier and stepped out onto the balcony overlooking the courtyard. A breeze swirled the perfume of orange blossoms while star energy streaked the night sky with purple, pink, and blue.

At the faint fragrance of winter pears, I turned. Ava approached from a bedroom on my left. She wore a bright pink spectralfiber tee shirt and shorts.

"Can't sleep?" she asked.

"Not yet." I kissed her cheek. "Apparently, you can't sleep either."

She snuggled against my side. "I keep thinking about Karis's brother."

"When we get home, I'll do some research. Maybe something will pop up."

"You won't do anything illegal, right?"

With a smirk, I shrugged. "If I get Bran's approval, it's not illegal."

She sighed. "I don't think it works that way, but I appreciate you doing what you can for her."

"I don't know if I'll find anything," I said. "Things differ from planet to planet."

Nodding, she nestled her head on my shoulder. She felt perfect in my arms.

Words swelled inside, but I hesitated. Was this a bad time to share how I felt? She was worried about Karis and her brother. Maybe discussing our future together should wait. Maybe it was too soon. Six months wasn't a lot of time to get to know each other, but I was sure and had been for months now. The small bag in my pants pocket was a testament to how I felt.

Glancing up at me, Ava wrinkled her nose. "What's got you all tied up?"

"What?"

She gave me a half-smile. "Your wolf is agitated and insecure. What's going on?"

I kissed her temple. I was signing up for a lifetime of being unable to keep secrets from her. There wasn't anything I wanted more.

"I love you. There's no one I'd rather be with, and you're more than I deserve." I pulled the small bag out of my pocket and shook the delicate ring into my palm.

The facets of the three channel-set red heartstones glittered in the low light. I'd picked two rectangular gems with a smaller gem between them to represent our past, present, and future.

Ava gasped. "Blaiz?"

"This might seem fast, snowdrop, but I know what I want. I want a future with you, one where I show you every day how much you mean to me. I want to laugh and cry with you, explore the world and life with you, fight and make up with you. Will you marry me?"

One hand covered her mouth, and tears streaked her cheeks while my heart thudded in my chest. She threw her arms around my neck. "Yes," she said. "I want that, too. I still have to pay off my life debt, though, right? It's only fair."

With a shared smile, we set about paying it down, one sweet, lingering kiss at a time.

Interested to learn where or why the Kali are disappearing? Keep reading for a sneak peek of *All the Poisoned Hearts*!

Escape. Rebel. Rise...or the fairest will die.

On the planet of Ramilion, the desert empirium of Itsavden is in upheaval. The empir is dead, resources are scarce, and Eirwyn's stepmother, Empirya Thana, hates her as much as the native Kali she uses in her neural manipulation experiments.

Princess Eirwyn should be the empirya, but a strange curse plagues her. When Thana orders her assassination, Eirwyn seeks asylum in the neighboring empirium of Trivasha.

A delicate treaty is being brokered between the two countries, but second-born Prince Harrixon agrees to hide the runaway princess. As they search for a solution to her curse, an unexpected connection grows between them. Eirwyn uncovers the curse's remedy, but Thana's cruelty intensifies and the threat of war looms. When a malicious attack endangers others who have protected her, Eirwyn must choose: disappear with the cure or die leading a rebellion.

Eirwyn's heart, life, and kingdom are in danger. The hunted princess must decide what—or who—she's willing to sacrifice to survive.

All the Poisoned Hearts

Izzy

Ten days to two months—that's how long it took to die from
starvation. One didn't just go to sleep and not awaken. The
whole process began with hunger pains and then progressed to
weakness and irritability. The final stage involved hallucinations
and convulsions before the heart finally stopped.

I pushed away the dark thoughts as the farming community
came into view. Its hushed stillness caused a lead ball to settle low
in my chest.

No one worked in the fields, and white desert sand coated clay-bricked patios and mounded near doorways. Primitive
houses of bleached wood and cracked clay clustered together, the
property boundaries marked with uneven lines of spindly trees.
A ladder leaned against one house, the roof's hole a gaping cav-
ity. The only movement came from several threadbare curtains
fluttering from open windows.

I pulled down my headscarf and squinted through the heat
haze. Was this the work of Empirya Thana or had famine claimed
the village?

My steps quickened, but Liam Balint, the chief security tech-
nician, put out a hand to stop my progress.

The transport bot trailing us rattled to a standstill. Fifty loaves
of wrapped bread waited in its cargo hold. Fifty small loaves that
would stave off the village's hunger for a few days.

I turned to Liam. "It-it looks abandoned."

Which made no sense. The native people here, theKali, clung
to the land they'd lived on for generations. They grew sour
melons, rope beans, and a grain called quamrah, perfect for
Trivasha's desert environment. But for the last few years, the
drought made it difficult for anyone to grow anything.

I frowned. "I was here just last week. They were celebrating the birth of a little girl."

Why had the industrious village residents vanished? If Empirya Thana was behind their disappearance, I'd... My lips twisted. I'd do nothing, like I always did. Despite my efforts, it seemed my monthly trips to the outlying communities made little difference. Numerous villages needed help, but on each trip I could only offer aid to a few with the bread I coaxed from the palace kitchens. Since I refused to ignore the Kali or allow them to struggle alone, I did what I could without the backing of the throne.

Liam's hand drifted to his holstered weapon, and he took several steps toward the center of the village where more skinny trees struggled. "Princess, perhaps I should go in first. Make sure there's no threat."

Before I could respond, two males shuffled into view, their arms full of farming tools as they headed for a nearby garden plot. Pastel tones of green, lavender, and blue shaded their silvery exposed skin. I released a quiet breath. The Kali were still here. "No need, Liam. Everything's fine."

As we reached the first house, movement caught my eye. Well, maybe not fine. A young adult female sat in the doorway, her body swaying back and forth like a metronome. Her glazed, dark eyes fixed on the white sand dunes shimmering under the fierce suns. While she continued her rhythmic rocking, several children gathered in the shade at the corner of the porch. Their lavender and green cheeks pale, they stood listless and unmoving like the White Saint statues guarding the Trivashan gates.

Although the community endured, a sense of wrongness threaded through the settlement like a silent predator. I shaded my eyes and walked closer.

"Princess Eirwyn," Liam spoke in an undertone. "You're running out of time."

The double suns hung overhead, their heavy heat baking through my headscarf.

With a sigh, I tucked a midnight curl out of sight. There were two remaining villages further out, but I'd have to get them next time. "Yes. Thank you, Liam."

An elderly Kali farmer emerged from a nearby clay-block structure, a worn, printed tunic and matching pants draping his emaciated frame. The suns had intensified the greens and purples on his grayish cheekbones. While his white circular forehead tattoo was typical, the elaborate design marked him as a village elder. He approached us with a brief nod.

"How can we help you?" The thin rasp of his voice held confidence.

I stepped forward with a smile and gestured to the transport robot behind me. "We're from the Trivashan Office of Domestic Affairs. We have wrapped loaves of fresh bread." The rich, yeasty scent curled around us. My mouth watered. I'd skipped breakfast this morning to avoid facing my stepmother, Thana, over the dining table.

He eyed the robot. "Two deliveries in a week?"

I blinked. "Um, we were unaware of a previous delivery."

"A large shipment of apples from the West Gardens two days ago," he said.

A pit yawned open in my stomach. Thana was up to something. It was the second village to give such a report.

I plucked my white cotton gloves away from my sweating palms. "If you've no need of the bread, we can take it to the next village."

"No, we can use it. Put it over here in the shade." He led us to a large, slate-roofed well covered with a thin wooden lid.

Liam and I unpacked the bot's storage compartment and stacked the bread loaves on the well's cover. The Kali was a hardworking, busy race, regardless of the weather. But while

Liam and I chatted with the elder, the children drifted away, and the two males with the farming tools left. Only a solitary male emerged from his house, his movements slow and awkward as he struggled with the sun shutters hanging off the hinges.

The elder's question drew my attention. "Any news of more water being delivered?"

"How are your water levels?" I asked.

His dark gaze remained steady. "Our well covers our drinking needs."

But nothing else. My heart sank. In the small plots of cracked earth next to each dwelling, sickly yellow plants wilted in the suns' glare.

"Empirya Thana's looking into possibilities." I hoped. I put the last loaf on the mounded pile of bread and closed the compartment. "We're expecting a solution soon."

The man nodded. "Many thanks for the provisions. May the Moon Goddess show you her goodness."

We waved and headed back to our dark blue wanderer. The sleek, teardrop-shaped vehicle hovered a foot above the sand, the Trivashan crest on its side gleaming. I looked back, noting the Kali elder still watched us. I fidgeted with the cuffs of the gloves I had to wear. With my bare hands covered, I couldn't break or ruin anything. Of course, there were always other ways my curse could manifest itself. Not that I wanted to discover them all. My stomach knotted.

Once we moved out of earshot, I turned to Liam. "Why would Thana feed these communities?"

Frowning, he pushed the button releasing the wanderer's access ramp. It whispered to a stop in the sand, and the bot rolled up the incline and disappeared inside. "Sebastian might know. But Princess, don't go digging into this."

My stepmother held no love for the Kali, and she did nothing on a whim. "I can't ignore starving, struggling people, Liam. They're Trivashan citizens. And this charity isn't like Thana."

Liam pressed his lips into a thin line, the wrinkles on his forehead deepening.

I touched the wanderer's driver's side door. "Can I drive?"

He gave me a measured look before nodding. "This time. Happy birthday."

Rolling my eyes, I climbed in. Unfortunately, flying home would probably be the most enjoyable thing about my birthday.

Liam settled his muscular frame into the passenger seat. In the last fourteen months, he'd become a surrogate father to me. He shared stories of when he and my father had been mischievous children, listened to my plans for when I became empirya, and taught me how to pilot the small hovercraft after Father's death.

Sometimes I dreamed about climbing in one and leaving my problems far away. But if I did, I'd never become empirya or discover how to cure the curse that made normal life impossible. I couldn't give up hope.

The vehicle rose high in the air, abandoning the rippling dunes of white sand below. Through the tinted windshield, the sky was a hard blue brushed with faint swirls of color. Brighter at night, the stardust swirls were energy particles littering the atmosphere. Stardust energy powered everything in the Duo Soles system, and the mining waste created a unique work of art every day. I switched on the Aerial Traffic Screen. Only a few smaller craft occupied our area, although traffic increased as we flew northeast toward the Spire. I gave the stardust energy freighter plenty of space as I flew by.

"Could you remove this trip from my security record?" I asked Liam.

"Are you sure your charity trips would disappoint Empirya Thana?"

I glared at him. "Pretty much. Please remove it. I'm returning with plenty of time to prepare for the party."

He tapped the display. "Plenty of time? Hidaya wanted to meet with you two hours ago."

I mentally winced. My best friend and assistant had not been pleased about my cancellation this morning. But the Kali were more important than a silly party. "It doesn't take that long to put on a dress."

Surrounded by white stone buildings, the Spire rose tall and glittering above the city. The intertwined glass double pinnacle thrust into the sky. Four smaller glass towers, two on each side, caught and reflected the sunlight. The structure looked different now with the rock glass platforms and bridges Thana had installed a year ago. I didn't care for the additions, but the attached walkways made it easier to visit my friend Davin. After the medic's semi-retirement, he lived in an apartment on the west side.

My father had turned to the physician when my strange physical symptoms started five years ago. Water would grow cloudy at my touch, or a vase would break as I walked by, or bright sparks would fly from my fingers. After every test had shown no sign of a mysterious illness, my BioDock had been examined. The device implanted in my forearm had revealed the typical basic setup, a biochip communicator augmented with a tracking chip. Davin turned to journals, medical logs, and mystics, hoping to uncover the root of my curse. The gloves were a mere stopgap, and Davin continued to look for answers in obscure libraries and ancient texts.

To my left milled a crowd waiting to take the Ramilion portal to one of our sister planets, the round gate glowing orange with transport stardust energy. The white stone wall and the park with its three reflecting pools flashed beneath the wanderer as

I flew nearer to the Spire. After I parked the vehicle near the hangar, I pulled off my scarf.

Liam jerked his head. "Go on. I'll log us in. You need to find Hidaya."

"Thanks." I gave him a grateful smile and hurried toward the main entrance.

I didn't recognize the two security personnel flanking the massive double doors, but I offered them a smile anyway. The younger one on the left blinked and blushed, his red cheeks brilliant against his snowy uniform. The man on the right turned and placed his palm on the identity pad. With a hiss, the wide glass door glided open. In the entryway, bleached columns soared to the vaulted roof. Sunlight streamed through the countless tall windows and played across the white-on-white patterned tile. My boot soles squeaked as I climbed the short staircase.

My steps slowed. There was no way to avoid the Microbiome Disinfecting Unit Thana had installed last month, citing concerns about "microbiome health." The metal MDU occupied most of the space at the top of the stairs, although a small passageway to the left allowed people to exit.

With a deep breath, I stopped under the silver hood. At the high-pitched whine overhead, I squeezed my eyes shut as the pipes released a rain of disinfecting particles. The mist landing on my bare skin left a greasy film behind. When the gate swung wide, I escaped into the hallway with the smell of strange chemicals trailing me. I didn't allow myself a full breath until the MDU was left far behind.

The Nav-Cat 3000 sensed me as I passed the airy throne room. The floating disc held a foot-high, floating hologram of a servant holding a map. "Welcome to the Trivashan Spire. Access the direct—"

I batted the Nav-Cat aside and continued past the library full of lower-level advisors, a couple of dining rooms, a theater and concert hall, and the busy kitchen. My destination, the study, waited near the end of the hallway. Once inside the dim room, I allowed the tension to ease from my shoulders.

No surveillance cameras, no advisors. My stepmother rarely stepped foot in the room. A control pad was mounted to the right of the doorway. With a gloved fingertip, I touched the button to open the solar shields covering the windows. Daylight flooded the ivory walls as I opened my BioDock to request a meeting with Hidaya.

Rows of rare leather-bound classics gleamed in the floor-to-ceiling bookcases. I'd read the stories of brave knights, valiant peasants, and lonely royals. Someone would slay the evil dragon, and they'd live happily ever after.

Too bad real life didn't work that way.

I settled into my father's favorite chair and pulled a folded square of origami paper from my pocket to work on until Hidaya arrived. It was a little difficult with gloves, but I'd become adept at completing most tasks while wearing them. It was safer for everyone.

From memory, I completed the folds, transforming the flat paper into a three-dimensional pinwheel. Like me, it turned and whirled but went nowhere.

A buzzer sounded, the noise louder than a Trivashan wasps' nest. "Hidaya here, for the princess." My best friend's voice was overly formal, required by Spire protocol.

I spun the pinwheel, letting it wobble and flutter in my hand. "Enter, please."

Hidaya walked in, her tall, slender figure complemented by the glistening Solknit uniform. "What the suns was so important that you couldn't meet with me earlier?" She looked up from her BioDock and gasped. "You haven't even showered yet, have you?"

Settling deeper into the chair, I gave her a sheepish grin. "It's not a big deal. It only takes ten minutes to shower and another ten to put on—"

"As your assistant, if you're not prepared, it makes me look incompetent. And as your best friend, I want you to enjoy tonight. There'll be plenty of eligible men arriving to meet you." She offered me a bright, encouraging smile.

Eligible men. I suppressed an inelegant snort. "I don't want a husband."

When my father grew sick, he signed a document decreeing my coronation after my eighteenth birthday. Although my birthday celebration was tonight, Thana refused to talk about an enthronement, my coronation, or any future arrangement. Still, I was prepared to rule Trivasha, even if my father wasn't alive to see it happen.

Grief swelled. My fingers tightened, inadvertently crumpling the delicate pinwheel. Opening my hand, I smoothed my paper creation. Permitting Thana to control Trivasha was incomprehensible. Marrying and living far away in a foreign land, unimaginable. I clung to the hope that after my party, Thana and I could discuss my future.

Hidaya perched a hip on the desk and squeezed my shoulder. "Kethiran is always with you, you know. Have fun, flirt, dance. Perhaps we'll both find eligible men, and they'll whisk us away on a thrilling adventure of undying love." She punctuated her statement with a fluttering of eyelashes.

I couldn't help but smile at her drama. If I could pretend this whole party was a simple birthday celebration, it might be bearable. But I knew something Hidaya didn't—Kethiran had forgotten me a long time ago. I was cursed and powerless, and Thana's patience with me grew shorter every day.

Hidaya consulted the list and bit her lip. "Um, you're scheduled for a hair melanin injection therapy in fifteen minutes?"

My blood freezing, I shot to my feet. "What? I never agreed to that."

"You know how the empirya is. It's all white, all the time, especially for parties."

Empirya Thana's odd preference for white had become well-known in the empirium. Clothes, hair, skin—it didn't matter. Hidaya, with her pale blonde hair, was lucky. Until now, I'd managed to avoid Thana's procedures and adjustments. Which was just as well, since I was dealing with my curse symptoms.

I frowned at my dark hair curling over my shoulder. "Could you dye my hair instead? Like, right now?"

Her look was understanding. "Sure. We can do it in my room."

The study door opened, and my stepmother swept inside. Her platinum hair matched her silk jacket and the floor-length gown. Ice-cold blood drained from my veins to pool in my stomach.

She offered Hidaya a genuine smile before her shrewd gaze raked over me. "Hello. I'm sorry to interrupt your meeting. I know concentration is a struggle for you, Eirwyn."

I schooled my features into a blank gaze, refusing to respond.

Thana's smile was a blade, her eyes glittering. "I finished early. We'll do the injection therapy now."

Her words sent my heartbeat racing. Cautionary stories of underground markets offering that sort of thing abounded—a quick injection for a different color skin or hair, another for temporary scent additives, still another for better night vision. But last week, Thana's assistant had given one of the kitchen staff a "routine treatment" in the lab. The woman returned to work being unable to speak. She'd recovered but still stuttered occasionally.

Thana continued. "Your mask and shoes arrived this morning. They're being delivered to your room."

"Mask?"

Thana's pale blue eyes went wide. "Oh, I didn't mention it? This is a masquerade party."

Of course. During the planning stage, I'd expressly vetoed the idea. I didn't want all the intrigue and scandalous behavior a masquerade party created.

She laced her fingers together. "The women will all wear masks to add to the mystery of finding you. The men can choose to forgo masks but will be wearing their formal whites with their empirium crests stitched on the outfit. You can use that identifier if your wit fails you."

I bit my tongue so hard it hurt. Long ago, I'd learned to avoid her verbal games. She won—every time.

"This is the perfect opportunity for you to find a husband tonight, Eirwyn."

"No, thank you. I'd rather not marry a stranger."

She pursed her lips. "As imperial leaders, we often must do things we'd rather not do for the good of Trivasha."

I took a deep breath, prayed for composure. How would my marriage to a stranger help Trivasha? Then I remembered the Kali's need for water. Maybe we could broker an agreement with Isvora, the sister planet we exported our water from. A marriage to one of the Isvoran empirs could lower our prices.

Thana waved a thin-fingered hand. "Come along. Everything is ready—"

The door swished open again, and General Valerian strode in, his beige balaclava leaving only his eyes visible. Four bars of silver on each shoulder of his military jacket glimmered. His coat flapped wide, exposing the weapons holstered at his waist and the wicked dagger strapped to his thigh. Before he pulled his headgear down around his neck, he pierced me with a leering once-over. I pretended not to notice.

"Your Celestial Majesty. Celestial Daughter." He bowed low to both of us before giving a curt nod to Hidaya. "I've received promises from the Purists. They will honor your request for a peaceful evening of festivities."

The rebel organization had killed my mother six years ago for using smuggled stardust energy. And now Thana was working with them? My blood heated. "Why are we cajoling promises from terrorists who murder our people?"

Valerian shot a glance at Empirya Thana, then me. "Princess, despite the Purists' questionable past, they only deal with Kali dissidents now."

A complete lie. "The Kali are Trivashan citizens. They live here believing they'll be safe. The Alard Agreement we signed decades ago promises them land, safety, fair treatment."

Thana's voice sliced through the taut silence in the room. "They're black-blooded animals, outsiders bringing their savage culture and dangerous beliefs to our safe empirium—"

I interrupted her. "*We* are the outsiders. They've always lived on this land."

Her lip curled, as if I was an infectious disease under her microscope. "Trivasha must move forward, away from outdated ideas and conventions. The Purists and their extreme methods are often necessary."

I barely heard Hidaya's sharp inhale over the pounding in my ears. Furious words waited like cornered animals, but if I unleashed them, Thana would lock me in the dark room. I swallowed hard as memories surged forward—choking shadows, unidentifiable rustling, or pregnant, tense silence.

Thana offered a thin smile to Valerian. "You're dismissed, General. I'll wait for you in the lab, Eirwyn." She turned and left, expecting us to follow.

General Valerian trailed her out, ever the faithful dog.

A heavy silence filled the room. My heartbeat pounded in my chest, as if threatening to explode. With trembling hands, I closed the shields and left the sanctuary of the study. I couldn't hide—my tracking chip made that impossible, and the punishment would be an hour or two of black, terrifying misery.

Hidaya's worried eyes studied me as we walked toward the elevator. "Maybe it won't be that bad, Izzy," she said, using my childhood nickname.

A sour taste climbed my throat. I smoothed the cuffs of my gloves. "Don't leave me. Please. She won't dare try anything with a witness present."

Frowning, she nodded.

The elevator deposited us on the third floor. Three hallways branched from the small alcove. The right and left hallways faded into the background because Thana's lair, the gleaming silver office suite, loomed at the end of the hall. The corridor stretched before us, the harsh recessed lighting illuminating every corner. I fought to control my breathing.

As we reached the entrance, the doors whooshed open, and my shoulders tightened. Hidaya squeezed my hand, the pressure of her fingers disappearing as adrenaline flooded my system.

Thana's office stood empty. She waited in the attached lab to the left, studying a computer screen. As the lab's glass doors whisked open, the smell of disinfectant swamped me. I squinted against the bright light and shining steel.

My stepmother's gaze met mine, and I shuddered.

We entered the lab, and Hidaya settled on a brushed chrome seat against the wall.

Thana's pale blonde eyebrows rose. "It's unnecessary for you to stay."

"It's entirely no problem, Your Celestial Grace. Princess Eirwyn doesn't feel one hundred percent, and I should stay in case she takes a turn for the worse." The lie tumbled from Hidaya's lips with ease.

Thana shot me a speculative look before she patted the matching brushed chrome seat in front of her. "Hmm, if you're not feeling well, I'll just do the bare minimum."

I sat and took a deep breath. It stuttered out in a wavering stream. I tried again. This was my first procedure here. It couldn't be that dangerous. One injection of Thana's special blend of stardust energy, and my hair would turn white—never mind I had no idea what blend she'd concocted. I squeezed my eyes shut, unable to convince even myself.

Now would be a perfect time for my curse to kick in. The strange symptoms changed every month, more freakish anomalies to add to the already long list. My most recent phenomenon? Disappearing into thin air, like the military spies trained by General Valerian. Recruits needed six months of training to learn how to use the elemental Class F energy which bent light. I'd developed the ability instantly. It had happened a week ago, in Hidaya's room. We'd both been speechless. Maybe if I disappeared now, I could escape this nightmare.

My thoughts stalled as Thana held up a syringe filled with clear liquid. Her fingers brushed my nape before sweeping my dark hair back above my ear. "Relax. This is only a pain reliever. Perhaps here above the ear...you'll feel a prick."

There was a sting above my ear, and the medicine hit my system. I clenched the metal armrests. The drug exploded through my body like a liquid punch and slammed my head back onto the headrest. My surroundings shimmered, no more substantial than a mirage.

Before I could draw another breath, Thana's icy fingers shoved my head down. An unexpected jab burned my nape. I jerked away, the serum a stinging fire. Tears welled, blurring Hidaya's horrified expression. My stomach flipped, cramped, and a rush of heat climbed my torso. Lurching forward, I vomited onto the antiseptically white, domestic Trivashan tiles.

Hidaya was at my side in seconds. "I believe Eirwyn is too ill to continue, Your Celestial Grace."

My stepmother's voice came from far away as she handed an item to Hidaya. "Give her this anti-nausea medication in five minutes. It will help her recover. She can return for her injection therapy when she improves."

The words sent internal alarm bells clanging as Hidaya helped me from my seat. If the injection she'd given me wasn't to change my hair color, what did it do? My emotions spiraled like an out-of-control wanderer. I fisted my hands, the seams of my gloves pressing into my sweaty fingers.

Thana pressed the intercom button above the counter. "Morana, activate the cleaning bot."

A ceiling panel slid open, and an eight-foot-long steel tube descended. A hatch on the bottom opened as it hovered above my mess on the floor. With a quiet whirr, it vacuumed everything up before spraying the area with a disinfectant. As the robot finished buffing the tiles to a high shine, I shuffled to the door.

A stronger person would've fought back, refused the treatment. And then I would've been punished. The door to the nightmarish dark room glared at me from the far corner of her office.

Hidaya's steady hands led me down the hallway. My head throbbed, a sour taste on my tongue. My clothes hung heavy on my skin.

As we waited for the elevator, Hidaya turned to me. "Suns, Izzy, I'm so sorry."

I was sorry too. "I need to lie down."

"Let me know if you have any other side effects, okay? I've never seen an injection site on the neck. Do you—" She hesitated.

"Do you want the medication she gave me?" She held out a small beige tablet.

Hidaya dropped it into my palm as I tried to work up the courage to swallow it. While one side was plain, a line of miniature letters decorated the other side. At a closer examination, a tremor ripped up my spine.

It was my name. The miniature letters marched over the tablet's plain beige face before they blurred into smudges.

Why would she inscribe my name on a simple tablet?

"No, I-I can't." I had no idea what Thana had injected into me, and I didn't want anything else the monster had made for me. In my current state, the possibility of the punishing dark room looked preferable to suspicious medication. I pretended to take it and mimed a swallow for the camera mounted near the ceiling. Once in the elevator, I buried the tablet in my pants pocket. I'd toss it later and pray Thana never discovered my deception.

Nausea swelled and subsided in waves. An ache built in my head, clenching my skull with vicious fists. When we reached my room, my friend helped me out of my soiled outfit and into a loose tunic. Curling up on the bed, I allowed my tears to slip onto my pillow.

Want to read more? Buy *All the Poisoned Hearts: A Snow White Retelling* on Amazon or wherever books are sold!

Glossary

- directed energy weapon (aka DEW): a handheld weapon that propels stardust energy with a force great enough to stun or kill

- drift panel: a floating gurney

- flare: fail spectacularly

- flixer: an animated photo

- hoarfrost: mild curse

- hoverchair: a chair that levitates above the ground

- ice cadet: a derogatory name for someone who's unintelligent

- Kali: a native race of people on Ramilion with pastel shaded skin; known for being magically gifted

- Kethiran: a spirit deity, known as the powerful, eternal creator of the Del Soles system

- laced: a process involving gene augmentations and splicing

- laserscreen: multifeatured screen that allows software programs to run simultaneously, as well as feature holograms, schematics, and 3-D displays

- milfoil glow: a hot-tasting spice, usually sprinkled on the top of barzina

- barzina: a creamy caffeinated drink, tasting of vanilla and other spices

- paszec: an animal with a huge fluffy tail that's a blend between a dog and a rabbit, kept as pets

- physipad: a medical device used to remove pain and diagnose injuries and illnesses

- quarkhead: a jerk

- Restorscreen: a moist protective covering for wounds and injuries

- shadowool: a wool known for retaining body heat

- solar: fantastic or cool

- Solknit: fabric similar to spandex, but more comfortable

- spectralfiber: thin, wispy fabric perfect for hot climates

- star steel: steel blended with star energy

- suns/suns' halo: mild curse word or phrase

- sunspotted: crazy

Book reviews are one of the best ways to support indie authors. Reviews can boost a book's exposure, so it's suggested by Amazon and shared by Goodreads.

If you enjoyed *All the Wild Hearts*, please consider leaving a review on Amazon, Goodreads, or even your own personal blog (if you have one). Thank you so much!

Writing an Easy Book Review

Writing a book review can be hard, but it doesn't have to be.

Review Template (pick one):

Not sure what to say? Just copy, paste, and fill in the blanks! Your review can be as short or as long as you like – but every word helps this book find new readers.

Option 1: Quick + Easy

I really enjoyed [Book Title] by [Author Name]. If you like [genre/theme], you 'll love this. My favorite part was [a scene, a twist, a character]. I'd recommend it to anyone who enjoys [similar books/authors or vibes].

Option 2: Feelings First

[Title] made me feel [emotion: hooked, heartbroken, hopeful, etc.] I couldn't stop reading because [reason]. I especially loved [character/scene]. I can't wait to read more from this author.

Option 3: Vibe Reader

If you're into books that are [adjective: dark, romantic, twisty, cozy, fast-paced], this one is for you. [Book Title] gave me major [vibe: fairytale, dystopian, small town, enemies-to-lovers] energy.

Option 4: Combo Review

I loved [Book Title] by [Author]. It was a(n) [adjective] tale that left me [emotion]. I loved [scene, character, twist] and can't wait for more from this author. If you like [similar book/vibe], check out [Book Title].

Also by J.M. Hackman

Series

- All the Poisoned Hearts, a Snow White retelling (Stardust Hearts Book 2) coming soon!

- Spark (Book 1 of the Firebrand Chronicles)

- Flare (Book 2 of the Firebrand Chronicles)

- Burn (Book 3 of the Firebrand Chronicles)

Anthologies

- Entwined

- Mythical Doorways

- Tales of Ever After

- RealmScapes

Acknowledgements

This story wouldn't be possible without the unfailing support from my family. They are my rock. Thank you for your love, your patience, and for pretending not to notice how often I talked to myself while plotting.

Thank you to Literary Pearl Editing for their expertise — all the mistakes are mine.

A warm thank you to Savannah Goins, Desiree Williams, Laura Zimmerman, Carrie Anne Noble, and especially Jebraun Clifford whose eagle eyes caught my flubs.

A heartfelt thank you to my readers—for every moment spent reading, every review, every share on social media, every word of encouragement.

And lastly, thank you to my Heavenly Father, the Author of all stories.

About the author

J.M. Hackman, the award-winning author of the Firebrand Chronicles and the Stardust Hearts series, loves thunderstorms, fuzzy socks, and thick chocolate milkshakes. Her engaging fantasy and soft science fiction stories are threaded with hope and end with a happily ever-after. While her characters are fearless, J.M. is afraid of spiders, wasps, and the crowds at post-Christmas sales. When she's not writing, she reads, crafts, watches football, and adventures with her family in the mountains of rural Pennsylvania.

Go to her website at www.jmhackman.com to learn more about her and to take the quiz, "What Book Trope Are You?"